Immortal Touch

Immortal Touch

ETHAN PEASLEY

iUniverse, Inc.
Bloomington

Immortal Touch

iUniverse books may be ordered through booksellers or by contacting:

iUniverse
1663 Liberty Drive
Bloomington, IN 47403
www.iuniverse.com
1-800-Authors (1-800-288-4677)

Because of the dynamic nature of the Internet, any web addresses or links contained in this book may have changed since publication and may no longer be valid. The views expressed in this work are solely those of the author and do not necessarily reflect the views of the publisher, and the publisher hereby disclaims any responsibility for them.

Any people depicted in stock imagery provided by Thinkstock are models, and such images are being used for illustrative purposes only.

Certain stock imagery © Thinkstock.

ISBN: 978-1-4620-7356-6 (sc)
ISBN: 978-1-4620-7355-9 (hc)
ISBN: 978-1-4620-7354-2 (e)

Library of Congress Control Number: 2011962415

Printed in the United States of America

iUniverse rev. date: 02/10/2011

Dedications are supposed to be heartfelt and difficult to write, and this dedication stays true to that thought. I went back and forth on this dedication, but I finally decided to stick with my original person.

This book is dedicated to the girl who doesn't know how much she means to me. In the relatively short time that I've known her, she's shown me that she is truly a beautiful person, not only on the outside but on the inside as well.

Introduction

I was not unlike most of your kind in my mortal years, always chasing after the girl I thought was the one for me, pining for her to say yes to my various—and vastly numerous—advances, staying up late to ensure that my work was complete, or drinking the home-brewed slave's wine with my fellow humans at the end of the night. Then, in my immortal years, when darkness kissed my lips with its velvety tongue and granted me sweet eternity, it all changed. I cared little for the girl, whose succulent lips and gorgeous eyes would fade into those of a haggard old lady if I did not feast from her first. The work my masters had given to me seemed so trivial and unimportant in hindsight, and in fact, the masters of society themselves became mere puppets to my very will. They would soon work for me in ways they couldn't imagine.

It is quite common for the mortality of man to be in the minds of the very creature it concerns most. I pondered this when I was alive. My closest friend and confidant did as well, and we both found that people spend the majority, if not the entirety, of their lives preparing for that one day when their heart stops, their vision fades, their bodies crumble, and they become just another feast for the maggots and worms that will no doubt infest their grotesque corpses the first chance they can.

My name, for those wondering, is Asael, and while I was once a man a vastly long time ago, I am now a vampire. Yes, the supernatural, the undead, a creature that goes bump in the night, a parasite among the *Homo sapiens*, the next step in the great evolutionary cycle, or as some of my wiser and spiritual brothers and sisters would say, the final part of God's will. Whatever label you wish to choose matters little to me, as I am what I am, and that is all. I drink blood merely to stay alive. It no longer gives me a great thrill or ecstasy like it did so many years ago, like it does for some other sanguinarians, and unlike many before me, I enjoy my immortality and the creature I have become.

Book One

The Turning

Chapter One

The darkness that surrounded my mind slowly broke, and when I awoke from my dazed slumber, I was a slave. I had had bad luck in a military campaign and was the property of my enemy. All fall from grace eventually, and it seemed Lady Fortune had spun her wheel and left me a broken shell of the warrior I once was.

A local merchant bought me shortly after I arrived in the great city of Rome. He needed a bit of a pick-me-up, if you will, financially. This raven-haired, fair-skinned dealer of death, with eyes of icy cobalt and a thick, greasy mustache, was a vile and disgusting mortal who deserved nothing more than death. His sins were not those of gluttony or envy, but of lust. Not the lust of a woman or even a man, but of children. He was notorious for buying child slaves, forcing them to do whatever he or his guests wished, and then laughing as they begrudgingly did so, with tears in their eyes. His only saving grace was that he knew how to utilize the adult slaves he bought, and thankfully he gave me the "honor," as he called it, of fighting in the Colosseum.

Gladiator matches, which throughout the years have been portrayed as magnificent duels between men and beasts, are a terrible spectacle to behold and are in no way the glorious things portrayed by your kind. One man dies, without honor and far from his homeland, while another gets to live one more menial and mediocre day. The surviving slave or warrior rarely gets anything good, and in fact, my own "master" decided it was a good idea to whip and beat me for every flaw or mistake I had made in the Colosseum, even though I came out the victor. It was through this very practice, his incessant beatings and lashings, that I became a machine of death and torment whenever I entered the confines of the ring. No man or beast could hope to stop the killing machine I had evolved into. My scarred flesh and deadened nerves had made me impervious to feeling the pain that plagued us, a fact my enemies would learn all too well.

Though the matches were not a glorious thing to behold, viewing me in the bouts was a rare sight indeed. My skill and grace with my chosen weapon became unmatched as I garnered win after win, my style akin to the waves of the ocean, strike after strike hitting the opponent until he finally succumbed and drowned under my constant assault.

It was here, in the fires of the Colosseum, where I met the sweet parasite that would change me forever. She was a medic of sorts, the perfect profession for our kind, and she was beautiful, with tantalizing olive skin and gorgeous emerald-green eyes that shone in the light of the moon.

While I was skillful, even masterful, I was far from invincible, and I would be forced to visit her numerous times, requesting bandages and water. Each request was met with a vivacious smile and a quick nod. Her touch, the delicately soft embrace of a wondrous vixen, worked miracles upon my wounded body. Whenever she was done with me, I felt more like Caesar himself and less like a slave.

I can remember after one session, she followed me back to my modest quarters. The barren walls and dirt floors were barely illuminated by a single meager torch. I had a thin layer of cloth for a bed. All I can remember of that night was that she was ravishing.

I remember her beautiful olive skin and amazingly green eyes, her ebony, silky hair shining in the torchlight. She left me completely and utterly stunned as she looked upon me, her gorgeous features working a magical spell that left me deaf and dumb to the rest of the world.

"Asael ..." she said, sounding as if she were about to break into tears. "I have something I need to tell you."

It was with that very sentence that she began to explain everything to me. She explained her supernatural heritage, her unending thirst for the blood of humanity, the completely undeniable cravings, and how her coven needed to grow with the fresh blood of a new member. I didn't believe a word of it at the time, but I loved her, needed her, and in an attempt to make her feel better, I pretended to believe and act excited as she told me the swarm of what I thought were lies dripping from her mouth. Sadly, it seemed, the ruse failed to work.

"I know it sounds crazy, Asael, but I swear on my unbeating heart it's true," she said, her green eyes boring holes into my soul, leaving me to shift uncomfortably at her unwavering stare.

Goose bumps seemed to infest my skin as a single breath of a breeze drifted through my room, alerting me to the already ice-cold flesh that was standing before me. I wanted to believe her, but it seemed like madness.

She smiled, somehow sensing my thoughts and feelings. Her brows furrowed, her teeth biting down upon her lips, and then finally her smile faded. Without a word, she grabbed my hand, her cold touch giving me chills as she pressed my hand to her chest. There was nothing there. No warmth, no heartbeat, nothing. With a look of genuine surprise, I gazed deeply into her sage eyes.

A bloody tear rolled down her cheek. She had finally found someone who believed her. Apparently, she had been trying to find a companion to bring to her coven for decades, but all ran away or attacked her when they discovered what she was, their screams being silenced and replaced by the crying moans of their murderer.

"I can help you escape, Asael. Leave this mundane life of servitude. You can be strong and powerful, and silence entire populations or raise an army of powerful acolytes. You can leave this place and never come back, travel the world and see things that need to be seen, that haven't been seen, and will be lost to the sands of time forever. Please, allow me to make you what I am, and break this wretched loneliness that has plagued me forever. Asael, be my savior from the darkening madness that has been slowly stalking my mind for years," she said as she held my hands, her soft, cool touch giving me goose bumps, her lips pressing down upon them, giving me a gentle kiss as she stared into my wanting eyes.

I was lost for words, something that generally didn't happen and hasn't happened in some time. I can only remember nodding like a fool at her offer. She smiled, and that smile showed her teeth growing into incredibly sharp fangs. Her green eyes became luminescent violet, shimmering and glowing in the light of the torches. She moved passionately toward me, her hands caressing my neck as she moved in as if to kiss me. Her lips brushed my own for a mere second, and then fell to my shoulder, her teeth piercing my skin and my crimson blood slowly seeping out of my body. It was euphoric, to be completely honest, and I wanted the moment to never end, but almost immediately after it had started, it was finished. She smiled as she backed away slowly, my blood leaving small streams at the corner of her mouth. I remember clawing at her, trying to make her come back and give me more of the sweet sensation that was her suckling my blood, drinking from me and giving me the waves of pleasure that washed over my mind.

A few minutes after being bitten, however, I began to feel what can only be described as death. Some of my kind will tell you that becoming what we are is highly painful, and if you survive the ordeal, you will always remember the immense and incalculable pain that you felt and where the torment originated.

For instance, my heart stopped, and from this crucial and vital organ began to pulsate a terrible sensation. The blood in my body stopped flowing, stopped pumping, and became stagnant. As I fell to the floor, a symphony of laughter came from my beautiful friend. She gracefully walked over to my dying body, cut a small incision on her wrist, and raised it to my mouth.

"Drink, my sweet Asael. Drink, and remain as you are forever," she said.

I sat there like a baby cub, drinking the delicious nectar that became my champagne, my everything, and the more I drank, the more she moaned in ecstasy, her head rolling back and her body becoming tense, her back arching and twisting as she felt the pleasure ripple through her. Her other hand clawed at my back, it was really quite incredible, this delicious pleasure we felt. Her bloody ambrosia truly did taste better than anything I've ever experienced, the finest delicacies paling in comparison. I yearned for more, and if I could have, I would have drunk her dry, but sadly she pushed me away.

My glorious friend looked drained of all strength and stamina. Her luxurious olive skin turned to a sickly pale white, her green eyes became a disgusting cold gray, her hair was not as full as it had once been, and in fact, bald spots that I had not noticed before began to appear in great number the more I gazed upon her. The more I observed her, the more this strange mix of awe and disgust bubbled within me, and she must have sensed this feeling, as she began to cry. Her tears stopped quickly, as I embraced her and kissed her passionately, showing her I did not care that this was her true appearance, the appearance that reared its head after not feeding or after she turned a human into one of our kind. She pulled up the hood that was attached to her cloak, concealing the hideous yet strangely intoxicating creature she had become.

"It happens to the oldest of our kind. When we don't feed, or when we are drained of blood for various purposes, our bodies begin to show signs of decay. Our hair recedes, our skin loses color, and our bodies become mere husks of what they once were," she said, her beautiful features slowly returning as she suckled on a passing rat. I'm not sure what it was, but something inside me changed. Yes, I was no longer human, but it wasn't that, dear reader. Her grotesque appearance slowly bothered me less and less, and it was as if that were the new definition of beauty, my new Calypso, and the longer I gazed upon her, the more and more the desire for other women left me.

I nodded, bringing my hand, which became icy cold almost instantly, to her face, caressing her perfect features. *Was this all that life was?* I asked myself. *Was this how I was meant to spend eternity, in a slave quarter with my Calypso?* If it was, it was more than fine with me. Sadly, this would not be the case, but at the time, I enjoyed every second of her presence.

Time passed by slowly, as it tends to do in the presence of the one you love. Minutes felt like hours, and we stood there, gazing at each other, not allowing simple words to cheapen the undying love we had just spawned for each other. Tragically, this only went on for half an hour, as my master trudged through the door, drunken and in a foul mood.

"You … Egyptian. Leave my slave … he has things to do," said the filthy merchant, his greasy mustache twitching as his lips moved to form the vile words that dribbled out of his mouth. Anger bubbled inside me as he told my beautiful Aphrodite to leave. Her eyes fluttered over to me, speaking volumes without actually uttering a syllable. She wanted me to kill him, to feed from him, and free myself of his wretched existence once and for all. Though I wanted to, I could not bring myself to do the task, to kill him once and for all.

Nafretiti understood my predicament, and patted my head lovingly. Without speaking, she filled my mind with the courage and ability to end the wretched existence of my master. Without worrying about any of the consequences, I descended upon him. I'm not sure if it was the knowledge I had that he could not stop me, or the dark voices that currently swim within my mind, but with unnatural speed and agility I clutched the insidious drunk with claws that had grown at my command. His heartbeat, which became my new favorite sound, began to quicken. His vile mouth opened and he let forth a scream of agonizing pain and horror.

"You. Merchant of despicable things, of death. Your retribution will not come slowly enough, your agony not painful enough. Sadly, I shall have to settle with your blood slowly being drained from your body, your flesh burnt and fed to your pets, and your palatial estate burnt to the ground." The words leapt from my mouth, as if inspired by an unknown force. My hand gripped the dirty man's throat as I lifted him into the air, like a rag doll being played with by a child.

With sweet silence flowing from his lips, I pierced his flesh with my fangs, breaking into arteries and draining him of his blood. His frothy, decadent red blood entered my mouth, and I could feel my strength increasing. I looked at my goddess, her lower lip quivering in her desire to partake in my feast. Her mind, open like a door, screamed out in thirst as I smiled at her, handing over my kill.

Her teeth ripped new holes into the man's flesh. New arteries were broken, and more of his delicate blood was drained. Her hair, which was slowly coming back on its own, regained its full body, and her skin became soft and flawless once more. Her eyes turned once again violet as she fed, but subsided to green shortly afterward. There she was, my Egyptian goddess, my savior, my Calypso. She flung the dead merchant to the floor as he became nothing more than meat for the dogs. Her face, which a few moments ago held a look of pure ecstasy, had turned to a serious expression that was hard to read. I knew she was neither angry nor saddened, but the look would always return whenever she had information to give me, a story to share, or a comment to make.

"The sun will be rising soon. Have you heard any of the vampire lore?" she asked, her silky voice filled with urgency.

I shook my head. I knew that vampires drank blood, and that was roughly it. I knew they walked the earth immortal, and that they were powerful. Other than that, my knowledge of them was nonexistent.

"For the first few centuries of your life, the sun will be able to instantly kill you. In fact, it is the *only* thing that can truly kill you. Our kind is truly immortal, and we do not die. Period. Our bodies may wither, but our souls survive. We are forced to linger in the netherworld, in essence the hell that so many humans sing about. And yes, before you ask, Satan does exist, but only a few have dealt with him.

"The lore, which is partly true, dictates that vampires sleep during the day to avoid the power of the sun. Our coven has decided to retire in a stone structure not that far from here. We can discuss more later, but just for right now, let's get to a safe place. We can return here in the nights to follow," she said, grabbing my arm as she led me to the river that divided the dead merchant's property. Her mind was bombarding me with powerful images and thoughts, half sentences and words that meant little me, but when all were heard and seen, painted a masterpiece that explained where we were going and more.

She seemed tense, almost frightened, as if she had done something wrong and was now trying to cover it up, like a child blaming a broken vase on the wind. My lips moved, forming words, but no sounds escaped. I remember wondering what fear was infecting her, which in turn infected me. When she finally decided to explain herself and her actions, we were far away from my new birthplace, my once dungeon and prison.

We were deep within the forests. The delicate smell of earth and leaves assaulted my nostrils as my newly augmented sense of smell became known to me. I once found the smell of earth and leaves pleasant, but I now found the odor sickeningly strong. My lovely Nafretiti turned around, and with bloody tears, began to explain her fear.

"There is a cardinal rule among our kind. Humans are never to be turned unless they deserve it," she said, her eyes looking down in shame.

"Deserve it?" I asked. My voice was low and dark, filled with a questionable hatred, as if I knew the answer to my own question.

She shifted her weight, sighed loudly, and began flashing images of various men and women in her head. Men and women who gave me a sense of dread and terror; men and women who had a newfound authority over me. The images drifted from her mind into my own, my new vampiric heritage gifting me with new abilities. With a weak voice, she began to explain.

"Humans who have done a terrible thing, such as genocide or showing vast amounts of greed, are turned into our kind to teach them humility. They must confront their sins.

"Some call it a 'dark gift,' but in reality, it isn't a gift … it isn't really anything. I sentenced you to an eternal hell on Earth. I knew you would perish in the arena and didn't want that to happen. I couldn't take knowing that the only person I had ever loved would die tomorrow. My unbeating heart melted at the very thought of it," she said, tears of blood rolling down her cheeks.

My feeling of hatred evaporated like a puddle as I embraced her, wiping away her tears and telling her everything would be all right. After consoling her, and of course stealing a passionate kiss, we walked for a little until we came upon a massive crypt that I had not recalled seeing before. It was completely made of stone, and appeared to be naturally occurring, as no work of tools showed on the rock that composed the walls. The only artificial piece on this monolithic crypt was the door, which was made of heavy iron and slowly rusting away.

We entered the mausoleum, the stagnant air being embraced by the subtle scents of perfumed skin and stale breath, used to feed the vampires within. The stairs that led to the very pit of the crypt were unnaturally steep, and it felt as if only the undead could traverse the path that led to the deepest bowels of the ancient resting place. I began to burn with a strange feeling of excitement as my lovely guide led me further down. I tried to the best of my ability to mimic each step she took. Each move she made, I attempted the same. It wasn't until we hit the final step that I saw the glimmering light from a single candle, and the feeling of excitement quickly evaporated, replaced by a very real feeling of terror and dread.

From the darkness of the shadows erupted the voice of an ancient being.

"Welcome, Asael. Today you leave the light of the living and enter the dark of the dead," said the disembodied voice. "Though you do not deserve our blood, it has been shown to me that you will be needed in the later years of this world."

The second the last syllable flew into the air, the disembodied voice took form. His skin was as black as night, his eyes a bright blue. When he walked into the light of the candle, I saw that he was bald, and covered from head to toe in tattoos of unknown origin. His body was wrapped in a loose-fitting cloak, the white linen draping over his skin. His satin voice gave me a calm, serene feeling, putting me at ease with my surroundings and situation.

"I can feel within you many questions, and they will all be answered in time, trust me," said the vampire, his words reverberating in my ears, playing over and over again in my head.

I was filled with a strange sense of pride the moment I saw this elusive and beautiful creature. He was as ancient as time itself, the oldest of our kind, but he was humble. He didn't want the vast amount of power or knowledge he possessed, and a glance into his eyes showed that it burdened him.

"Nafretiti, does he speak?" asked another vampire jokingly, his blue eyes staring at me. I could feel his presence within my mind, could sense his personality and demeanor, and could see that he had never done anything wrong to those who didn't warrant it. I could feel his caring, gentle touch telling me everything was going to be all right, that even among monsters and beasts such as we, there were decent creatures.

Nafretiti smiled and nodded at them. She looked at me with a smile, mouthing the words "speak." She sent images of calming oceans and valleys to try to settle me down. I felt like a child, and in truth I was one. I had tried to speak, trust me I did, but no sound would leave my stubborn lips, no sentences would form, no thoughts entered my mind. I was, for the first and last time ever, intimidated. All I could summon the strength and nerve for was a bow, and a quick and gentle one at that. I noticed the gentle vampire move in closer, his arms becoming entangled around my neck, an odd attempt at what felt like a hug.

"You are among friends, Asael," spoke the blue-eyed, light-skinned vampire.

He truly was gentle, and very friendly, something I needed at the time. Something, I think, he knew I needed. I can't explain how I knew, but I could feel that he would be more of a mentor to me than Nafretiti or the ancient one ever would. I already felt a camaraderie with him, a strange feeling I had never experienced before.

I smiled. It was the only reaction I could summon. The blood of my new existence raged through my veins, and with this strengthening blood I grew more confident. I was still weak, still an infant in comparison to those around me, but that night was the last time I would feel weak.

Days had passed after my first meeting with the immortals. The tattooed one and Nafretiti vanished for that span of time to have a discussion about my turning, probably to scold her on breaking their one real rule, but the conversation has forever and will forever be clouded in mystery to me. The others of the coven seemed distant and cold to my existence, and they abandoned me in my infancy. That left me and the fair-skinned, blue-eyed vampire alone. This is how I learned of our heritage, and how we came into existence.

He was dwelling within a dark corner, his eyes scanning the ancient page of an unknown scroll. He was mumbling to himself, lips moving a mile a minute as he scoured the page for knowledge and insight into a matter that was dear to him.

"Can I ask what it is you are doing, Mordecai?" I asked. My questions, in the first few years, were always very brief, and to the point. It would take decades until I became a better orator.

He looked at me blankly. His blue eyes neither passed judgment nor did they show contempt, they just stared at me, studied me, as I awaited his response.

"I'm reading about our history, Asael. How and why we came into being. It is something all of our kind should know and understand," he said, his eyes returning to the ancient text that was our past.

The scroll, which was rather plain and not decorated in the slightest, seemed to resonate with a divine voice, as if whispering to those around it to take heed of its warnings and lessons. Its dark whisper soon became an echoing song as it filled my head with pictures and sentences, which once put together, painted a very confusing picture.

"Who is Cain?" I inquired.

"Our father. The patriarch of the entire vampiric race, and the first murderer," replied Mordecai, as if he were recalling a fact repeatedly spoken to him when he was younger. "Care to hear the story?"

I nodded with enthusiasm as I took a seat next to him and

prepared for the images swimming in my head to begin to make sense. Mordecai prepared to tell a story that he wished to make perfect. He spoke with the skill and grace of a wily politician, moved like a graceful ballerina, and when he was finished, I was entranced with it all.

"Cain and his brother, Abel, had been told to give an offering to their God. Cain, being a farmer, gave the Lord his harvest as an offering. Abel, a shepherd, offered the Lord the very finest of his flock. Favoring his brother's offer over his, Cain became enraged and slew his brother. The Lord, having discovered the fate of Abel, questioned Cain. He cursed Cain with a mark, or our curse of drinking blood, and told him to leave.

"Cain, who by this time was undergoing his first death, was growing more and more famished as time went on. Meat didn't satiate him, drink didn't quench his thirst, and nothing could satisfy his overwhelming hunger.

"It was around this time that Cain underwent a hallucination. He claimed an angel came down to him and told him that if he drank the blood of his fellow man, he could live. Cain, after refusing to break and give in to the illusion, broke down and attacked another human. With unknown strength and speed, Cain attacked any who were around him, drinking rivers of blood that filled his empty vessel with divine satisfaction. It was here, from this first assault, that he created the very first of our kind. We arose, from the shackles of death, and with our new Father, drank our fill," he explained, his blue eyes growing misty as he reminisced.

"Where is Cain now?" I asked.

"You have met him, Asael. He was the very first to greet you into this lovely crypt, after Nafretiti, of course," answered Mordecai, a smile coming to his face as he revealed to me that the very vampire I respected and admired the most was in fact the very same person I was to thank for my existence.

Cain, the ancient vampire, father to all vampires and the first murderer. At the time, I was amazed that someone so humble and modest could be the very thing that sired so many strong creatures. That someone so powerful and wise could be dwelling within a rocky crypt, instead of palatial estates filled with the greatest delicacies this earth had to offer.

"I can sense what you are thinking, Asael, and there is a reason for it. Think of it this way—Cain sticks out in crowds. His jet-black skin in a sea of pale faces? His inhumane pigment, darker then Egyptian or Nubian skin, would be a sure sign that something was amiss with this fellow. If he did not hide, he would be hunted, and killed," said Mordecai, his revelation as to why Cain hid made perfect sense.

"You know as much as you have to know about all of us, yet your life remains a mystery to me. Tell me about yourself," Mordecai said, his blue eyes shimmering in the candlelight, his cheerful expression shining through.

I was filled with an awkward and strange sense of apprehension. What do I tell him? That I was once a strong warrior who failed miserably in my mission and became captured by the very enemy I had sworn to destroy? Or that right after I was inducted into this eternal brotherhood, I killed the one thing that haunted and plagued my years of bondage? I stammered, my head swimming with lies I could tell, fabrications I could create to give a better story, but Mordecai would know I was lying.

"I'm ... I'm not sure where to begin, I'm afraid," I said, my mind racing as I began to remember the murder of my greasy bastard of a master. I quickly understood that there was no use in lying; Mordecai had at the time the ability and power to read my thoughts no matter how strong I tried to resist, so I found myself confessing everything.

"Tell me, Asael, what were your mortal years like? Before you were brought to Rome," said Mordecai, his blue eyes shining with curiosity.

"Before I was forced to Rome," I corrected him. "Well, I was a warrior. I was fast, agile, and strong, and my leaders knew that I put a swift end to all those who opposed me. When I was a child, before my military years, I often would watch my heroes come back from battle, and would pretend to be them, fighting the various children around me until I was the victor.

"One battle, one disastrous, terrifying battle, I was sent with a group of fellow soldiers to investigate the whereabouts of the enemy. It was supposed to be simple, quick, and above all, easy. It was sadly none of the above," I said. "What we saw not only horrified me and my men, but it became burned within all our minds. We saw figures, the silhouettes of men, slitting the throats of prisoners and enjoying the warming liquid that cascaded from the incision. I know now that these *things* were not men, but in fact, vampires."

"They couldn't have been vampires," said Mordecai simply.

"Why do you say that?" I asked.

"We are the only ones, at least to my knowledge. Cain is the father of vampires, and he claims that we are the first of his children, and so there could be no other vampires. They could've just been men drinking the blood of those they captured, but they were not vampires in the way that we are vampires," he answered.

"In that case, these beasts in the skins of man were gruesome, and terrifying. Their numbers were limited, which was good, but they were the biggest men I had ever seen. They towered over their prisoners, dwarfed our tallest soldiers, and their physique was godly!" I explained, standing on a chair to get my point across.

This all brought a smile to Mordecai's face. He found my story entertaining in a way I did not, which infuriated me in a way I cannot express. He was making my final days of freedom into a joke, and that irritated me.

"All right, we both know of your days before bondage, but what of the days within bondage? Your grace and skill with a blade in the Colosseum was amazing. It was as if old god Mars himself blessed you with his prowess. Please, tell me of that time," he requested. The smile that once was on his face was replaced with a look of reverence.

"My mortal years of bondage … such a sad and depressing topic. Where to begin? I was once a slave to a successful, yet grotesque, merchant who delved in all sorts of things. Though he was successful, he always yearned for more money, and so he turned to a life of crime. His stalls, boutiques, and shops were all fronts for an amazing network of slave traders and prostitutes. He knew who to deal with, and who not to deal with, and because of this knowledge, he only dealt with those in power. Senators and guards, anyone who held power, would soon be suckling from my master's teat as he dished out whatever their fancies were. Children of all ages, exotic beauties from faraway lands, and even the occasional animal were all given away to tickle their desires.

"I was chosen from a small group of hopefuls. I was selected by my master to be his newest addition to his collection of slaves. He used me for cleaning the stables and keeping his horses in working order."

I averted my eyes from Mordecai's gaze, trying to hide my shame and contempt at what I once was. Mordecai saw what I was doing, and in a matter of seconds was already consoling me and trying to make me feel better.

"Thank you, my friend. It's difficult for me talk about my life as a slave. When I became less and less useful, not because of my age but because I realized he wouldn't harm me if I did nothing, he decided to put me in the Colosseum. I was forced to fight strangers who had caused me no harm, and wouldn't have caused me harm if their masters hadn't forced them to fight, either.

"My first duel, I remember, was preceded by the warm, tingling sensation of urine trickling down my leg, all my attention and strength trying to control my bowels in an attempt to not soil myself further."

Mordecai began to smile, and nodded. He was there at the fight, and remembered it fondly. He recalled the various dodges and parries I had done during the match, and remembered the "glorious" way I ended the poor soul that was my adversary.

"The way your wondrous blade cut through the soft flesh that was his neck, the falling droplets of blood singing as they fell upon the ground. Never has there been a more beautiful song sung. Simply and utterly amazing," said Mordecai, his face assaulted by an uncontrollable grin.

This vampire, my lovely savage, seemed to shake with excitement as I recalled my days as a gladiator. The way he finished my stories with his own account of the event, though at first flattering, became increasingly annoying. I had to stop him several times, and ask him as nicely as I could if he wanted me to tell the story. He apologized, and allowed me to continue.

"I hated the Colosseum. Fighting someone for a wrong they have done against you is a just cause, fighting to survive out of hunger is another, but fighting someone because they were pressured into a corner is barbaric and savage. I prayed for death every night," I said, the words dripping off my tongue as I spat them out with contempt.

"But, Asael, you were so good! I remember hearing the crowds and masses cheering your name and roar for you! You had to enjoy the praise and worship a little bit," said my vampiric brother, his mortal side shining through with the excitement of a child.

"You don't have to enjoy something to be good at it, my friend. I fought because if I didn't, I would die, and while I prayed for death, I would not be responsible for mine. It was a means to an end, the only means to a multitude of ends. If I didn't fight the best I could, my master would whip and beat me, so to stop the gruesome beatings, I mastered my art. I used the torture he instilled to help forge myself in the fires of pain," I said, my voice becoming cold and distant.

⸙

"I've told you what you wanted to know about me," I said quickly. "Now, if I may, tell me about yourself. What were you as a man? What have you done with immortality?" I asked, my black eyes studying him as he composed himself to speak.

"Sadly, my friend, I do not remember my mortal years. I've been told by Cain that I was a lonely man with no family left, wars and sickness dragging them away from me. He also told me that he took pity upon me, and wished to better my life by ending it," he said, a heavy sigh escaping him before he continued. "However, Cain did not fully understand the curse that his God gave him. He thought that by draining me of blood, I would remain dead. He was, however, vastly mistaken. I'm not sure who was more surprised when I awoke from the deathly slumber. Awakening from what seemed like eons of sleep, shaking the mortal coil once and for all, it was a strange thing to me.

"When the initial shock and hunger vanished, Cain was kind enough to tell me what I had accidentally become, and the various information that was required to survive. My life from then on, while long, has been rather uneventful," he said, nodding his head as one does when stating facts.

Something had felt strange with Mordecai's answer, that he had lived so long and yet done nothing with his time, but I let go of my suspicions as I saw Nafretiti enter the room, her glorious features embracing my sight as I could do nothing but gaze upon her. She walked, which was like a panther stalking its prey, toward Mordecai with an urgency that at the time was lost to me. Without a word she gazed into his eyes, and nodded her head.

"Asael, you have to leave," were the only words that left my mentor's mouth as they forced me out of the chamber, trying to save me from experiencing a tragedy I was not ready for.

Chapter Two

Thrusting me out into the darkness of night, my vampire brethren left me to my own devices to pass the time. They had told me nothing, gave no explanation, and because of that I was curious. In the short time that I had been a vampire, I had never been alone to myself. Others of my kind surrounded me— Mordecai with his gentle nature, Nafretiti with her passionate spirit and knowledge, and the sensations of Cain with his ancient wisdom and profound insight.

I felt like a child in a candy store. There was so much to do and sample that I became giddy with excitement. My feet, which seemed to have minds of their own, quickly carried me through the forests of green leaves and viridian grass to the outskirts of the nearest city, where the delicate sounds of humanity embraced my supernatural ears. The harmonious melody of voices sang out in a symphony as I approached, making my head swim with intrigue. Who would I meet? What would I do? All these questions floated into my mind as I gazed upon the world with new eyes.

"You look lonely," said a prostitute, attempting to solicit me for a nefarious illegal act that would end in her undoing.

I nodded at her with a wink and a smile, and inquired her prices.

She told me, and then tried selling herself further by saying she had the lowest prices in town. I remember finding that to be especially amusing, as it is usually the cheap ones who are the most disease ridden (Let that be a note for future reference.)

She led me into her dwelling, a modest little structure with a bed and hearth. Only the barest of essentials graced her walls. Once we had settled in, and the pleasantries dispensed, she began to strip down to nothing. I inspected, rather than admired, her body, finding various scars and flaws infecting its fair, rough skin. She suggested I do the same, but with a shake of my head and a large grin, I embraced her in my arms. The scent of her skin, a nice aroma of lavender and dirt, assaulted my nostrils as my lips skirted across it. I followed a single vein, throbbing with fresh blood up to her neck, and with instinct driving me, sank my teeth into the pulsating stream. With a whorish moan, her head rolled back in pleasure as I took my fill of her delicate blood, leaving nothing behind.

My eyes, returning from their predatory dilation to normal pupils, focused once more on her rough features. Wrinkles that had not been there now screamed for attention, her soft yet thinning hair became coarser by the second, and her eyes, which were what drew me to her originally, clouded with cataracts. The skin around her fingers clung to her bones and puckered up as the liquid blood dried up. Her tongue dried and shriveled, the various taste buds turning black and dusty. She would be the first of many dead corpses I left in my wake.

☙

"You enjoyed that, I see," said Nafretiti, materializing out of the dense fog outside of the prostitute's dwelling. "Isn't it magnificent when you take that first kill all on your own? When you finally throw away the shackles of mortal men and become a god?"

I remember nodding, her words running through the darkened alleys of my mind as I slowly came back to my senses, my latest kill making me feel a euphoric high. It sadly would be among the last euphoric highs I would ever feel.

"Whether we like it or not, we vampires generally try to cling to what once came naturally and easy to us. We are beasts. Don't let anyone tell you otherwise. The only difference between a wolf and us is that we can communicate with our food in their own tongue," she mused.

"Why are you here? Is there any reason behind this latest lesson?" I asked, not amused.

She sighed as she walked closer, the smell of death palpable on her newly tattered clothing. She flashed pictures of destruction and death at what was once our dwelling, half sentences and snapshots indicating who survived and who died.

"I was told to come and fetch you, my love. Cain wishes to speak to you, Mordecai, and me," she said, the images still plaguing my mind as her words crawled around my skull.

"What? Why? What has happened? You just barely told me to leave!" I exclaimed.

She smiled, the kind of smile a parent gives when their child does something cute. My vampiric life apparently mimicked her own. She too was sent away a few days after becoming a vampire to drink from the cup of immortality and do whatever we wished. She too drank from the blood of a street walker, and she too was told to return to her home to discuss something with Cain.

"Something terrible, my dear. Our resting place was attacked, and our coven is now left broken. Cain wants to make sure everyone is safe, and I fear the darkness that harbors us may become darker," she said, and without warning we were gone.

Cain stood before us, his cheeks soiled with the bloody streaks that his tears forged upon his face, his eyes swollen and puffy from mourning the losses he endured. He was a broken shell of what he once was, and the respect he once commanded had faded. His mind, against his will, flashed images of torment and torture, half sentences and full poems forging a path into our minds that crippled our muscles and ravaged our bodies.

"We were assaulted by an enemy we never saw coming. The only solace I can give is that he is now dead. Ephraim, our once friend and brother, turned on us and began feasting from the very creatures that were his family," explained Cain, streams of tears rolling from his undead eyes as he spoke.

The entire room fell silent. No one made a sound; for fear that it would send Cain into a flood of anger. No one had a thought, for fear that it too would cause Cain anguish. I remember standing there, silent, mourning a brother I barely knew. After what seemed like forever, I felt compelled to ask my burning question.

"But, Cain, I thought we could not die. That we were truly immortal."

Disgust and groans attacked me on all sides as the last words that dribbled from my mouth seemed to cheapen the moment. Cain, who had always been a pillar of strength, shuffled forward until he was face to face with me.

"There is one way to ensure a vampire never comes back," spoke Cain, his baritone voice echoing in the empty room. "If one were to imbibe all their blood, the victim of said act would never be able to return again.

"It is a rare punishment, Asael. We do not enjoy killing our brothers and sisters, but at times it is the only way to prevent their madness from spreading. The only way to stop the chaos they sow," he responded.

"Asael, you must understand," said Mordecai, the voice of

reason, "that we all have one trait that is passed on from generation to generation. Nafretiti becomes cold and calculating at will. Mine is my inability to let go of my humanity, clinging to it like a child to a blanket. Sadly, Ephraim, our maddened brother, had the trait of hearing the voices of those fallen. He communed with the dead, and their constant chattering drove him mad."

It all made sense, as if pieces of a puzzle were clicking together that had never fit before. I had always wondered why Nafretiti had called me "my love" one minute, and the next seemed strange and distant. Or why Mordecai, the second vampire to survive his first death, was more human than me, a new fledgling. But what did that mean for me? I heard the dark voices of those fallen, heard them crawl and scratch within my head, but I also was losing my humanity, becoming more and more cold and methodical each day. Only time could tell.

The group's fratricide of their companion shook them, and the unbearable silence penetrated me to the very core. I knew what they had gone through was indescribable, and no creature should ever have to kill their kin under any circumstances, but I began to grow restless with their grieving. I paced the dark corridors of our crypt, the darkened voices mourning the passing of the dead vampires. It may be insensitive of me to say, but the whole thing left me very perturbed. I thirsted for revenge on the mortals who destroyed my living life, yearned for the vengeance I would sow upon them, but nothing came of these feelings. No great adventure and no vengeance would be had. Yet.

The first to actually break from the nightmarish silence was surprisingly Mordecai, who came to my modest dwellings in the evening. His eyes, which were puffy and red with tears, peered into my own, which were dry. Anger rippled through his body as he saw my face, pristine and untouched by the bloody tears that infested his own. His fists clenched and his jaw tightened as his stare made me shift in my stance.

"You truly are Nafretiti's child," he said, the anger in his words biting me to the very core.

"I didn't know Ephraim, Mordecai. He was a madman who mumbled to himself and swung his arms at things that weren't there. I steered cleared of him, as I knew he was of no use to me. I can learn nothing from madmen," I replied, my eyes shifting from his.

He said nothing, though pictures of Ephraim rippled through his brain, as did thoughts of guilt. He didn't want to remain with the coven if they were going to kill someone without trying to help them first. It wasn't right in Mordecai's eyes, and it wasn't right in my eyes either. People should be given chances to better themselves before they are judged finally and wholly. While I disliked Ephraim, his punishment was unjust and far too permanent for my tastes.

Mordecai circled the room, pacing back and forth, mulling over a single question he wished to ask, but could never summon the courage. A single tear fell from his eye, but not from the pain that he felt from losing a brother, but because he was trapped in a place he did not wish to remain. Whether we liked it or not, we were shackled to Cain for a reason that eluded us. The farther we were from him, the weaker we became. It was infuriating.

"I wish to be free of the hold that our father has over us, Asael, be rid of all contact with him," said Mordecai.

"Why? Cain has done nothing wrong, other than order the

death of Ephraim, but he did that for the good of the coven. Surely you can see that, Mordecai. Do not let grief cloud your judgment, my friend," I said.

"Cain has many sins to answer for, Asael. The creation of our race, for one. The slaughter of millions because of what he has made us, that is another. He has also killed many of our kind for the simple reason that he did not enjoy their presence," replied Mordecai. The anger that had rippled through him before surged back.

"You know, Asael, there is a way we could escape the confines of this dreaded stone hell and have the same strength we have now without being near Cain," plotted Mordecai, his voice filled with a malevolent tone. "All we need to do is feed from him and kill him. Do to him what he did to Ephraim."

I was curious as to how Mordecai knew this would work, but his words excited me greatly. I had already begun to grow tired of the life we lived, always having to check with Cain before leaving our domain, or growing weaker the farther we traveled. When Mordecai told me his plan, I became a willing accomplice in the overthrowing of a once powerful mentor.

Anticipation and excitement coursed through my veins as we approached our patriarch that fateful evening. The air, pungent with the scent of Cain, filled our nostrils as we climbed the stairs to his chambers, his soon to be eternal resting place. Mordecai, who was usually filled with bubbly laughter and witty banter, was stone silent and uncharacteristically angry as we ascended the stairs to what could possibly be a quick death.

The doors to his room creaked as they opened, revealing a room filled with old scrolls and relics of unknown origins. We found Cain sitting at a large desk fashioned from various things found within the crypt, reading and studying his surprisingly vast library of scrolls and tomes, his fingers combing the pages with unbelievable speed and grace, pages being raped of their secrets and thrown to the side the second they were of no use anymore.

"Ah, Mordecai and Asael. Where is it you wish to go tonight?" he said, his jet black eyes peering into our souls.

His question was met with silence. Mordecai glared at Cain with a palpable rage, his newfound hatred for the vampire seething and emanating from his body and infecting the air around him like a disease. Cain rose from his seat and advanced toward us, his face filled with sympathy and genuine respect for Mordecai.

"What is it, Mordecai?" spoke Cain, his ancient claw grasping Mordecai's shoulder, like a father does to his son when giving sage advice.

The ancient vampire, not being satisfied with silence, ravaged our minds for the answers he sought. Every memory and thought we had was peered into and examined by the ancient, until he finally found the kernel of knowledge he wanted. Our betrayal was brought to light and my heart sank.

"You wish to kill me? To escape from this place and live life on your own? My death will not give you this, Mordecai. You know that," said Cain, his eyes piercing Mordecai. "My death will only bring oblivion to you and any who partake in the act."

I looked on in confusion as the titan of a vampire spoke to Mordecai. The belief that killing the first vampire would cure all vampires was a myth, or at least that was what I had been told in my short life as a vampire. It just simply did not work that way, though I'm sure it was attempted many times over. Why did Cain think that his death would cause our destruction as well?

"You know that is a lie, Cain. Your protector has left you for some time. You know he will not come back just to protect you, his lesson failing to change you in any way," snapped Mordecai, spitting as the last words left his mouth.

Cain's face did not change. His favorite child rose up against him, like Zeus to Cronus. The three of us did not move. Like stone sentinels, we merely gazed upon each other. After a few moments of this, Cain let out an audible sigh and fell down in his chair.

"You wound me, Mordecai. You have been with me longer than any other, and now you wish to leave. Why? Because of Ephraim? You are allowing your curse to cloud your judgment," said Cain, referring to his humanity.

Mordecai said nothing, but his mind betrayed him as it flashed his thoughts into our minds. He hated Cain, but it was a new hatred, not an ancient one that he had hid from anyone. Ephraim was the reason for his fall from grace with Cain, and whether Mordecai would admit it, he would have forgiven Cain eventually. But I, newly turned and already chafing under the regime of Cain, could not allow time to heal this wound.

I flashed images of hate and contempt in Mordecai's mind, fanning the flames of his anger to awaken the sleeping giant that was his fighting spirit. A low, echoing growl emanated from Mordecai as he glared at Cain, his blue eyes becoming a glowing violet as he allowed the beast within to come out.

Chapter Three

The doors to Cain's chamber remained open as Mordecai and I, invigorated from the death of our Father, danced with the corpse of Cain. His inky black blood covered the walls from the short fight he had put up, but due to fatigue and hunger, he didn't last long.

Cain did not enjoy feeding, he despised the taste of blood and because of that hatred did not feed for weeks at a time until he absolutely had to. It left him very weak before he fed. Easy prey for Mordecai and myself.

"You did it," I said, congratulating Mordecai on the Olympian task he just completed.

"But now what? What does eternity have in store for us? We killed Cain, a coward and a murderer, but the others loved him. Nafretiti loved him, and I'm sorry to say this to you, but she will not embrace you as her child anymore, Asael. We have to leave before the others discover what we did. They'll soon become like Ephraim, incapable of thought and crazed with instinct," said Mordecai, his hand clutching my tunic as he spoke.

"What do you mean? You don't think they'll savor and enjoy their new freedom? Leaving the clutches of Cain and embarking on a great new world?" I asked curiously.

Mordecai shook his head, sighed, and sat down on the steps that led to Cain's chamber.

"No, Asael, I don't. We didn't technically kill Cain, we just weakened him enough to sever the bond with him."

We were stronger and superior to our brothers and sisters, and I could tell that Mordecai was thinking this simple fact would stir a war among our kind. It was obvious at that point that we needed to leave.

It made sense, kind of. I won't pretend that I understood the stuff Mordecai was saying, and I apologize that I cannot explain it better. I understood that Cain was drained of blood and we were superior to the other vampires, and the other vampires may be affected, but I had no idea that Cain was that crucial to our survival. I knew that killing the first vampire was a myth, but questions flooded my mind, and no answers were in sight. Before I could ask any of them, Mordecai pulled me through the crypt and out the door, leaving my brethren and my love behind us.

The sweet scent of the trees wafted into my nostrils as we forced our way away from the one thing we had become used to, from the one thing that gave us protection and shelter. Mordecai's icy grip crushed my arm as he led me through the dense forest, the fallen leaves and undergrowth crunching beneath our heels. The darkened voices were abuzz with information about the area, which I related to Mordecai, who was apparently dead to their words.

I looked toward the black night sky, white specks of light piercing the obsidian atmosphere. As we advanced deeper into the forest we passed dying bushes and destroyed trees, the charred remains of a recent battle enveloping our eyes.

Time, which generally passes quickly for our kind, moved impossibly slowly that night. It seemed that we had been traversing our path for years before we finally came to a resting place Mordecai found suitable for our night. It was a small cave that had areas where it seemed unlikely the sun would touch. We couldn't be sure of this, however, so Mordecai offered to remain closer to the opening of our temporary new home for the time being.

"What is the plan?" I asked, excitement dripping from my tongue.

"We live. We survive. Pick a type and stick with it, I suppose. Become the best at what it is we must do," answered Mordecai, his voice plain and cold. "Tonight, the last night of our stay in this wretched place, will be our own time. Taste freedom, and drink from the cup of life."

Mordecai said he was going to visit a radiant maiden who was the servant to a general, a gift from a regent for distinguished service. He would not feed from her, but he admired her and observed the menial tasks she was put through. To be perfectly honest, his humanity was holding him back from being truly great, but such is the way of gentle giants.

My goal for the night was to visit the senator who lined my dead masters' pockets with his patronage. He was a paranoid man who erected great gates around his estate, manmade creations to keep unwanted guests such as myself out. Sadly for this senator, the gates would not work and would only further anger and irritate me. Before, my goal was only to inspire fear and feed from a servant or two of his, but the second I viewed these gates, my goal transformed into feeling his life ebb slowly away as I drank from the chalice that was his neck.

Breaking the bars of the gate like a chicken bone, I crept through the vibrant darkness that loomed over the sweet-smelling garden that surrounded his home. I found myself sneaking through the shrubs and groves that tainted the natural landscape, and finally came face to face with the entrance to the senator's domain. My icy claws clutched the handle to the front door, causing it to creak noisily as I stalked my way through the annals of his palatial dwelling, the gentle shadows bathing me in stealthy invisibility.

Laughter and heartbeats erupted into my ears as I snaked my way into the senator's main living area. I found it ornately decorated with glorious linen, silks, and guests who filled the room, each from a different background or walk of life, but none ever having been touched by poverty. The senator stood in the middle of the room, relating a story of Caligula and Neptune, whipping himself into a verbal frenzy as the anecdote spewed from his mouth.

To be honest, the story was a funny one, and his charismatic smile made me cling to every word as I snuck up behind that grotesque senator. Miraculously none of the patrons of his house saw me. My cold hand silently went up the powerful senator's back, finding the perfect spot to dig my claws into the spinal column that supported his body. When the spot was pinpointed, the sweet sensation of skin splitting sent chills down my spine. Screams erupted from the audience as I lifted the senator into the air, his grubby hands clawing at my iron grip.

His limbs went limp as I lifted him higher into the air, his blood dripping down into my gaping mouth as I savored the feeling of his bones crushing beneath my palm. The gallery of people merely stood in terror as they watched their host become the puppet of an unnatural beast they would never see again. Their horrified eyes met mine as my teeth impaled the supple neck of the senator, relishing the last of his blood before throwing him to the side like garbage.

The cacophony of terrified heartbeats was music to my ears, the sight of them trembling in fear became burned within my mind like a great mosaic. The darkened voices swirled within my head, telling me to feast upon them all, but that would draw far too much attention to my existence than I wanted.

Before I departed the dead senator's house, I thought of maddening images and insanity-inspiring thoughts, driving the patrons of the house insane with the images that plagued their mind. The delicious sound of screams was the piece d'resistance to the joyful tune that was their heartbeats.

❧

Before continuing, I know some of you are probably pulling away from me, not supporting me like you might be supporting Mordecai. I understand the reasons behind this view, and want to explain that I, unlike Mordecai, am inhuman. My humanity began to die the second Cain's blood embraced my veins, enjoying Nafretiti's curse that she endowed me with to the fullest.

❧

Having had my fill of blood, I began my adventure to our resting place. Euphoria and ecstasy washed over me, not because of the recent feeding, but because of the simple fact that I had my freedom. I was freed from the shackles that Cain's regime had impressed upon me, freed from human law and obligations, and even freed from Mordecai if I ever saw the need.

The wind howled and the trees danced as I ran through the dense forest, skipping from fallen log to moss covered rock as I progressed. The stars above me shone and pulsated like beacons of light in the distance, illuminating the vast landscape. The mouth of the cave was coming up on the distance, embraced on either side by the rocky arms of the mountains, and a feeling of joy cascaded through my body as the notion of sleep danced in my mind.

However, as I entered our temporary habitat, the sounds of weeping enveloped me. Sitting upon a cold damp rock was Mordecai, blood staining his linen shirt and a tuft of long raven hair clutched within his claw. Bloody tears streamed down his face as he held the hair to his pale skin, mumbling the name of the beautiful servant maiden that he was going to visit that night. At that moment, I knew what he had done, and while my unbeating heart felt nothing for the girl it screamed in agony at the sight of a friend in torment.

"I … I killed her …" he muttered, his words being broken by gasps for air.

Darkened voices fluttered within my head, spilling the details of what had happened in my absence. Mordecai, who had always clung to the shadows when visiting the girl, had shown himself to her, her master believing he had unknown company. At first, everything was going fine. Mordecai was charming and chivalrous, but when the alcohol that had been served took effect within my friend's system, he became enraged and bestial. The servant girl's master, who was always abusive and unkind to her, hit the girl in front of Mordecai. Seeing this act of discipline sent my companion into a rage that didn't cease until the master's blood was in his mouth.

But the voices stopped after that. They divulged no more information, as if afraid to talk about what happened next. As if some taboo occurrence had taken place, and speaking of it would send them into oblivion.

"What happened after he died?" I asked, my claw grabbing his shoulder gently, ruffling the cloth a little.

He looked into my black eyes with beautiful sapphire orbs, and images of what happened danced in his mind.

"I drained the master, but tried not to swallow. It tasted so divine, so sweet, I couldn't resist the urge. My saliva had mixed with his blood, and in my drunken stupor, I embraced the girl and …" he fell silent as another blood filled tear fell across his cheek. "… I kissed her."

The darkened voices screamed out, their voices drowning out any other sound around me, but they offered no insight as to what was so bad about this kiss.

"I don't understand the problem. Perhaps you could explain to me why that is such a bad thing," I said, trying to not sound as ignorant as I truly was.

⚬⚬⚬

He sighed heavily, tears flowing freely from his sapphire eyes. He nodded his head, and breathed deeply. His mind, which before was wracked with grief, was now trying to remember exactly what happened.

"You don't know what happens to humans after we have kissed them after feeding?" he questioned, grief vacant from his voice.

I shook my head, truly ignorant of the consequences such an odd act might bring forth, realizing that Mordecai forgot how young I truly was.

"When our kind feeds, our saliva becomes toxic for a very short while. If a human is exposed to it, they'll grow infatuated with the vampire. Eventually, they will go insane with their infatuation. Cain always enjoyed calling them ghouls, completely willing minions in essence. Creatures devoted to the every whim of the being that made them.

"And to ensure that this terrible fate didn't befall the radiant mortal I loved, I ended her life quickly. Ghouls tend to mutilate themselves in an attempt to get the ones they love to care about them. I didn't want her to do that," he said, gripping the strands of hair even tighter.

"How did you do it?" I asked, all feeling of sympathy lovingly being thrown away from my body and being replaced by a sense of curiosity.

"I drank her blood. Making a ghoul goes against everything I stand for, and drinking from them was something Cain didn't like, so it seemed that it would be my only penance. Feasting from a creature who, before tonight, was a beautiful woman," he said, bloody tears flowing from him again as he pictured her within his mind.

"You did her a favor, Mordecai. In the end, these mortals will only be ravaged by time and live pathetic, worthless lives," I said, walking to my area of the cave to sleep, knowing full well that my words went against everything Mordecai believed in.

I awoke from a restless day of bad dreams to a night filled with wonder. Mordecai and I were leaving our old domain within the next few days, but before we did that, I had unfinished business.

Though Mordecai was convinced she would never speak to me after what I had done to Cain, I had to see Nafretiti one last time before I left. Her blood flowed through my veins, and leaving without so much as a good-bye seemed wrong. I also knew that if I didn't say good-bye before leaving, her voice would continue to crawl around my mind as it had been ever since our departure from the safety of the crypt.

After listening to the dark voices rant and rave, nuggets of truth seeped from their dead tongues. I finally discovered that Nafretiti was in a small town near the cave, and I immediately set out to find her. Thoughts raced through my mind as to what might happen during our encounter. Would she forgive me? Would she attack me? Would she beg me to return to the crypt? Questions with no answers thrashed my mind as I danced toward the town, joyously awaiting what could be my last meeting with Nafretiti.

The sweet aroma of townsfolk filled the air as I strode through the narrow streets, drinking in the miniature metropolis that Nafretiti had chosen to bless with her presence. The delicate sounds of hot metal plunging into water as blacksmiths worked late on orders mixed nicely with the foreign accent of a local merchant bartering with potential buyers. The subtle thrill of death embraced the place as well, the telltale sign of a vampire's presence.

The darkened voices beckoned me to an alley that was the perfect place for a blood succubus to dwell. The stench of rotting decay reared its ugly head as I ventured deeper into the darkness, and it was when I reached the dead end that I saw it. My Egyptian goddess, her features still as beautiful as the day she turned me into what I was.

"Asael? Is that you?" she asked, her voice filled with an uncharacteristic sadness.

I nodded my head, not saying a word as I remained awestruck at my glorious Nafretiti. Her face was red with blood, probably due to the mourning of her father, and her pupils were enlarged due to the ravenous hunger that she had been trying so hard to satiate.

"I'm surprised you even attempted to see me. We were all very angry at what you and Mordecai did to our beloved Cain. Though my anger has left me, the others still cling to their hatred of you. I think it is because they are afraid of what may happen to them if they thought for themselves," she said, her bloody claw rising to my face as she caressed my cheek.

She gazed upon me with a combination of anger and disbelief. We were supposed to be eternal lovers, never wanting the other to leave our side. But her fears and skeletons made her far too dangerous to be around. When Cain died, something inside her changed. She became a glutton for blood, trying to fill the void that Cain left in his eternal absence. Though I loved her, I had to sever all ties with her if I were to grow stronger as a vampire.

"Without Cain around, happiness is an emotion buried and trapped behind a wall," she snapped angrily.

"You've become weak, Nafretiti," I said coldly, my anger gripping my tongue.

It was at this moment I realized that she no longer was my Nafretiti, but instead a pathetic creature possessing the corpse of a long-dead Egyptian, clinging to the memories of Cain and his restrictive regime. She may have claimed to have forgiven me, but her mind screamed with rage and anger. It was when I saw within her mind that I knew Mordecai was right, and she could never be my Nafretiti again. She would never forgive me.

She must have known what I was thinking, for the rage and anger she was trying to hide from me boiled over the surface and she rushed toward me, her claws slashing at every inch of my being, her eyes filled with bloodlust. A small tear rolled down her cheek, regret wracking her insides as she clawed at her own child, madness ripping away her personality as she attacked me. I evaded all of her strikes, and her cuts were superficial. The blood of Cain ran through my veins, and I easily outmatched her.

My mind erupted in a cacophony of images of Mordecai and myself draining the ancient Cain of his blood, a successful attempt at demoralizing my once radiant love. Almost immediately, she began clawing at her head viciously, as if the images were a tangible object lying within her skull. Claws met bone in a gruesome attempt to pry open the dark prison that was her mind, only to have her claws break, covering her hands in bright red blood. I swiftly grabbed her by the throat, and brought her closer to me, her claws still frantically ripping hair and flesh from her skull in a vain attempt to pry the images out.

She never stopped the attempt to get rid of these images, even when my fangs punctured her flesh and began draining her of her scarlet plasma, the sweet blood bathing my throat as I savored every drop. She flailed this way and that, slowing down only once her body and mind became sapped of strength. Though it was not the way I wanted our engagement to end, I relished every second of the encounter, and when I finished I threw her corpse to the side like I would've any other meal, immortal inhumanity coursing through my veins.

I departed the night-covered alleyway and made my way toward the outskirts of town, finding myself near the graveyard where they hastily threw their dead. The wonderful scratches on the wood of those poor souls who were mistaken for corpses filled my ears as I danced on their graves, Nafretiti's blood empowering my curse even more. I clawed at the earth of a particular mortal, whose scratching was ferociously loud, and I laughed at the sheer terror they must have endured, their primal fear realized as their entire world sank slowly in the darkening madness of death that would overtake them. I began to dig up the grave of the terrified human dwelling in their casket, successfully clearing the area of earthen materials. I opened the wooden box that held the poor soul who might have died if it were not for me, and smiled widely at her terrified gazed.

She was nothing special in my opinion, though looking back, she was beautiful by mortal standards. Her hazel eyes stared at me for a few brief seconds, clear bewilderment filling them. When she realized she was saved, her arms wrapped around my neck in an effort to say thank you.

"How may I ever repay you?" she asked.

I smiled, knowing full well what I was about to ask had untold repercussions to the poor girl who was about to entertain me for days on end.

"A kiss, my dear. Your life for a kiss," I said, a charming smile spreading across my face.

Without a second's hesitation, she kissed me on the lips. Glorious fluid exchange. I grinned like a madman after that sweet kiss, sweet saliva sealing her fate. The toxic effects of my kiss after feeding took almost immediate effect, as she began to claw at me for another kiss, begging me to show some sign of affection.

I merely laughed, prying her iron grip around my neck away, and told her about a wonderful blue-eyed, pale-skinned friend of mine who would just die if I were to introduce her to him.

Chapter Four

Mordecai stood in awe, gazing upon the ghoul and examining every inch of her. Terror, sadness, and anger thrashed through his mind as he thought about what I had done. He looked at me with eyes full of rage, but behind that rage, I could sense joy.

"Why did you do this?" asked Mordecai, his humanity clouding his thoughts about the wonderful achievement I had just created.

I only smiled at my friend, saying nothing to appease him or offer peace of mind. The ghoul clung to my side, kissing my arm and hand passionately. The stench of earth and the decay of others still lingered on her clothing, but it suited what she was perfectly.

"Answer me, Asael. I want an answer. Why ruin her life?" he demanded, his pupils becoming enlarged with rage.

"I had to experience the process for myself, for an experience, either good or bad, is still an experience. I knew what and when to do it, but I didn't know the true repercussions of making such a pathetic creature. And besides, we will be leaving this wretched place soon for more exotic landscapes and richer bloods. If we cannot find food, we have the ghoul to feed from," I explained.

My answer brought a smile to Mordecai's face, though it quickly disappeared as he returned his gaze to the poor creature who clung to my side, groveling for affection and attention like a mangy dog. My hand combed through her hair as I noticed the attention that Mordecai was giving her. I smiled at how quickly his anger evaporated when he saw the poor thing.

"Where did you find her?" he asked, his hand caressing her cheek and brushing the dirty hair away from her eyes.

"She was in a graveyard. She, among with a few other poor souls, were scratching their caskets in a frenzied attempt to get out. I picked her grave because it looked the freshest, and her screams of terror were swimming inside my head like a wonderful song," I said, looking down at the pathetic ghoul who had begun to scratch drawings into her arm, the blood slowly trickling from the self-inflicted wounds.

Mordecai bit his lip at the sight of her blood, the clear need to feed washing over his face as the blood dripped on the ground. The moans of the ghoul filled the cave as she clawed deeper into her arm to siphon more blood to the surface, using the red nectar to scrawl portraits of me on the stone walls of the cave. I smiled at the wonderfully crude images, marveling at my creation with eyes full of paternal pride.

I squatted next to my lovely creation, grabbing her arm with both hands and bringing it up to my mouth. I suckled her warm blood from the gouges in her arm, my eyes rising to stare at Mordecai, who stood there hungrily lusting over the sweet champagne that was the ghoul's blood. I pried myself away from my creation, and offered her delicious life force to Mordecai. He was hesitant at first, not wanting to hurt such a lovely specimen of the human race, but his bestial need for sustenance overrode any humanity he held within himself as his fangs pierced the flesh of her wrist, the lovely taste of blood making him lust for more.

She didn't like Mordecai drinking from her, apparently. She hit him in various areas of his body, and even tried to pull away from my vampiric friend many times, but to no avail. I laughed viciously as I witnessed the terror the ghoul was being put through, and laughed even more when I saw Mordecai's disgraced look upon his face when he finished.

"Wonderful, isn't it?" I said as I patted my creation's head, smoothing out her hair as she lay on the ground, pale and weakened from the loss of blood.

Mordecai said nothing, but I knew he agreed with me. He knew his ways of clinging to humanity were impractical, and I knew deep down in my black heart that if he could change his ways, he would've. But such was his curse that he was incapable of thinking like a true vampire.

"It's not easy, Asael, not being able to feel normal because of the guilt you feel whenever you feed," he said, his hand wiping away the blood of the ghoul from his mouth.

"I know Mordecai, I know. Which is why I made the ghoul. So that you would not be inundated with this irrational guilt you have about feeding. Animals eat vegetation and other animals, humans eat animals, we eat humans. It is the way of our existence. Hopefully with my creation, you will not feel that way anymore, and instead enjoy the eternal life that has been given to you by the sweet embrace of darkness," I said, my hand rubbing his shoulder, trying to once again make him feel better.

The ghoul looked up with excitement, her eyes full of desire and lust. I beckoned her to come closer to me, and she obeyed like the beast she had become. Her heart beat faster as she edged her way toward me, her mind filling with impure thoughts. I grabbed her arm and pulled her closer to me, bringing my lips up to her ear.

"If you allow my friend to use you without any problems, I will allow you to become what I am. Is that a deal?" I whispered, my hand caressing her cheek as I awaited my answer.

Her head nodded eagerly as her hazel eyes stared at Mordecai, who was observing the encounter with great interest. She embraced me, and I in turn embraced her back, for she was doing me a favor that she had moments ago despised with great passion. Apparently, this humanly gesture I had given her amused Mordecai, for a large smile washed across his face.

"So, I get to feed from the ghoul when I wish?" he asked, his smile not leaving his face as he thought of the way her blood made him feel.

"Yes, though you have to conserve her blood. Ration it, if you will. You and I both know what happens to the fragile creatures if they lose too much blood at one time. Make this ghoul last," I answered, turning away from Mordecai as I stared at the portraits of me on the wall.

A note on ghouls, as I feel like now is as good a time as any. While at first they are entertaining to watch, constantly clinging to the master who made them and routinely inflicting pain on themselves as if it made our kind feel bad for them, unless they serve a purpose or were made for a special reason, do not make one. Mordecai was right to kill the ghoul he made on accident; they eventually become sickening creatures who mutilate every last piece of themselves until finally they die.

The night my ghoul finally killed herself was both a joyous one and a depressing one. No longer was I sadly swimming in a sea of affection and enduring clingy behavior, but on the other hand, no longer did Mordecai have a source of food. He had grown strong feeding from her every few days, and when she finally died from her wounds, he did not mourn her. I was very proud of the blue-eyed vampire.

"Mordecai, do you wish to talk about her death? I know that

you were closer to her than I was," I said, staring at my old friend as we lay in our den, waiting for sleep to wash over us.

His response, which was very surprising I'll admit, gave me a devilish sense of achievement.

"She was only a ghoul. No real loss in her death," he said truthfully.

I had finally, after what seemed like centuries of us being together, rubbed off on Mordecai slightly. My curse, to a degree, became his curse. He no longer viewed certain creatures as his equal, and that was one small step in the right direction. He, however, still moaned and groaned about tasting the blood of those he thought of as equals, but he no longer waited for weeks on end to feed. It was lovely to watch someone who was older than I finally mature.

After the ghoul died, and Mordecai was left to fend for himself once again in the world of feeding, he began to wonder how I dealt with my curse. How I remained undisturbed from the wretched thing that made me what I was, my apparent inability to connect with my prey in the way that Mordecai could.

"How do you do it, Asael? How do you remain numb to the problems of those you feed from?" he asked me, his words drowning in sorrow.

I didn't know what to say. Did Mordecai think I didn't struggle with what I was? In truth, I suppose I didn't. In all actuality, I probably enjoyed the thrill of the hunt more than any vampire before me. My friend stared at me, curiosity and sadness radiating from him, his blue eyes filled with bloody tears.

"I only remember the bad parts of my mortal years, Mordecai. The torture and pain I felt saturate my memories like a wet cloth. When all you remember is death and sadness, it is hard to mourn those who sustain you. It's hard to worry about the loved ones that they'll be leaving behind," I replied truthfully.

Mordecai nodded, but my answer apparently did not satisfy

him. He glared at me, wanting me to continue the conversation. It
was difficult for me, as I knew no other way of living.

"Asael, you always talk about how you despise the effects of
blood on us. The fact that it makes us into fools and gluttons if we
are not careful, yet you feed each and every day. You drink from
more humans in a week than I do in months. Why?" he asked.

"It stops the voices. That is why," I replied, my eyes now avoiding
Mordecai's gaze, bloody tears flooding my eyes, blurring my sight
and making things crimson.

"The voices? You mean you still hear them?" he responded in
disbelief.

In their youth, all vampires hear voices. They are those of
our kind who have died, and for some reason, decide to stay
and commune with fledgling vampires. The older our kind
get, the easier it is to block them out. But some vampires,
for whatever reason, never block them out. They hear them
scratching around in their minds, offering unwanted advice
and terrifying insight.

I nodded to Mordecai, a bloody tear rolling across my cheek,
leaving a crimson trail. My mind erupted into the images and thoughts
of the darkened voices, and I allowed Mordecai to look within,
seeing the ancient musings of our dead brothers and sisters.

"Drinking blood makes them dormant. Ephraim, before he was
killed, muttered that to me in one of his only bouts of clarity when
I first became the thing that we are. I am determined to not dance
slowly into madness and allow them to become legion within my
mind. Ephraim's fate will not be my own," I said angrily, the words
leaving a sour taste in my mouth.

Mordecai didn't say anything at first. His eyes fell upon me, studying me like an animal studies the movements of its prey. He edged his way closer to me, slowly and carefully, as if making a wrong move would send me into a tirade and I would attack him. I was considered, with the blood of Cain within my veins, an ancient of my race.

"You know, Mordecai … Cain refuses to forgive us," I said honestly and with sorrow.

I remained silent after that, but the anger bubbling within me caused my mind to send projections of Cain into Mordecai's mind, plaguing him with the conversations I had with him not so long ago. He heard with his own ears what was said, and it moved the vampire to tears. Crimson droplets of blood flowed like rivers down his face as he heard his mentor lament against him for what he had done. I did nothing to stop him from crying, only stood there like a fool, awaiting the tears to stop naturally.

He looked up at me, red smears covering his face, and through his eyes I sensed a huge weight being cast deeper into his unbeating heart. He never said so, but I think that was the night he forgave Cain for turning him into what he was. They were even, a life for a life.

"What is it like, Mordecai?" I asked, looking into his sapphire eyes. "Being able to relate to them. Knowing their fears and wants, desires and cravings? Do you enjoy your experiences?"

He glared at me, not completely sure if it was ridicule or curiosity that was motivating the question, but with a heavy sigh and a quick nod, he responded, "It's hell. It's like waking up each night and realizing that what you are doing, what you are, is wrong. We are parasites among a race of humble and weak creatures, but even more so I loathe myself … and if I had the courage and willpower, I'd walk into the rising sun and never look back.

"Each dawn, right before sleep comes and takes me, I pray for the ability to not see the terror-stricken eyes of the sad human I chose to take,"

Book Two

The Black Death

Chapter Five

Centuries passed since the untimely death of my lovely creation, and the world around us changed. Empires crumbled, tyrants rose and fell, and humanity evolved. They were no longer the civilized denizens of a shining utopian empire that conquered and shaped all, but instead dirty plague bearers who clung to the every whim of their lords and ladies in hopes of that shining utopia rising once again.

Though the humans fell into poverty and intellectual decay, our kind flourished. The bubonic plague, a dreadful disease spread by flea-infested rats, engulfed the continent like wildfire, and infested humans with the sweet presence of death. The pathetic creatures began dropping like flies, and those who weren't killed by the disease were feasted on by Mordecai and myself. We remained anonymous for awhile, lingering in the shadows of time and space.

The sweet scent of bodily waste filled the streets, as bodies piled into mass graves, loved ones disposed of like week-old trash. Limbs of the dead clung to the earth with a lifeless grip, their gray-dead skin laughing at the fates of those still alive. In all honesty, I felt sorry for the poor bastards who became infected with the deadly plague, and Mordecai was moved to bloody tears at the sight of children weeping for their dying mothers. These creatures were terribly afflicted with the various viruses and infections of their era. Though these infections flavored the blood of our prey, it was becoming ridiculous when out at night walking the streets, watching the terrifying lunatics preach about divine retribution and flogging themselves.

⁊

"We need to do something. Help them somehow," my blue-eyed companion said, his mind lingering on the pathetic creatures leaving loved ones behind.

"And how, Mordecai, do you plan to do that? Kill all of them so they don't suffer anymore? Make them like us so no disease can grace their fragile bodies?" I asked, all sympathy for the humans evaporating from my mind as I glared at my friend, my curse guiding my thoughts.

"We can feed off of the aristocrats and give what we take to the less fortunate. It will allow them to pay for any treatment there might be, or at least feed their starving family. I see no reason for you to be against this, Asael. You always say that upper-class blood was what you craved more than anything. Now is the time, Asael, feast upon them and do a good service for the humans. For once in your life, think about the ones you feed from," he said, his hands gripping my collar as he tried to beat his idea into my head, appealing to any hero complex that might lay dormant in me.

While not all mortals deserve to be saved, Mordecai made sense and appealed to my desire for blood. The aristocratic lords sat in their castles and estates, far from the vicious diseases that tore at commoners every day. My eyes squinted as I mulled the idea over in my head, my angelic companion staring back at me, his dirty peasant appearance hiding his devilish tastes. It was Mordecai's lot in eternity to work with those who suffered, feeding off of their plagued blood and learning of their trials and tribulations. He knew better than anyone what they craved, what they wanted, and he knew exactly how to give it to them, a quick death delivered by two fangs piercing their arteries, ending their suffering in a time that despised their very existence.

I nodded in approval, my mouth salivating at the thought of being unleashed upon the blue blood of Europe, my eyes glowing at the terror I would set upon them.

"Fine … I will feed off of the lords and ladies of this era, and you give away their valuables to the peasants you deal with. But I warn you, the second this becomes a burden and not an adventure, I will feast upon both classes, and the Black Death will look like the common cold compared to the destruction I shall bring," I snarled.

Mordecai smiled with glee, nodding his head slowly. His mind filled with images of salvation and praise. He still yearned for the acceptance of the pathetic race that we fed from, even though every time he revealed what he was to them, he would accidentally end up killing them in self defense. His mind would always become inebriated with the dreams of saving the lowly urchins of the street.

Mordecai demanded we start as soon as we could, and while I abhorred helping the humans, I yearned for a feast worthy of the lords that were my new targets. I made forcefully entering their dens my task, and feasting from their most cherished family member my pastime. While my leisure activities were enjoyable and fun, Mordecai punished himself by watching the creatures he grew to love the most suffer and wither away.

It wasn't just the terrible plague that entered their bodies and destroyed their insides, but tuberculosis and other horrific diseases slowly made them putrid husks. While I grew to find their presence outside of my feeding intolerable, I sometimes found myself weeping for those who were visited by death who did not deserve such a visit, only to have that trace amount of humanity ripped from me by my hunger.

Those who did deserve to die a putrid death, however, were another story altogether. The aristocratic bastards of the time deserved to be impaled upon wooden stakes and have their honor and titles stripped from them, their cowardice and arrogance making the title of noble nothing more than a false epithet.

We lingered in the darkened streets, listening to the various stories of the downtrodden and afflicted. Mordecai truly cared for them, showing genuine compassion and offering apology after apology to those who complained about the various problems that infected their shortened lives. I, on the other hand, only focused on their fears and hatred toward the upper class. I fed upon the madness that danced within each of them, the darkness that jumped frantically behind the mental barriers that prevented them from unleashing it.

It wasn't long before we discovered the tyrannical atrocities of a single aristocrat whose actions appalled Mordecai, instilling a biting rage within the soft-spoken vampire. Though this creature was human, I had a slight respect for what he did with his nobility, throwing away the unwritten laws of social society and taking whatever he wished for himself. Though I found the nobles of the era to be cowardly bastards, his bastardly ways seemed to be so refined and perfect, one couldn't help but enjoy them. We determined, however, that he would be the first to fall, the first of many blue-blooded cretins to meet their fateful end by my hand.

We interrogated a few more urchins, discovering where this tyrant made his den and various weaknesses that plagued him. Mordecai found the target that knew his dwelling, a filthy child with blond hair, yellow eyes, and teeth rotting within his mouth, his skin an unhealthy gray.

"Where does our lord go to at night to sleep, my boy?" asked Mordecai, his hand embracing the child by his shoulder. The child, not used to a friendly embrace, flinched as my friend touched him, expecting a beating for some wrongdoing. "It is okay, child, do not fear us. I just wish to know where the lord of this place lives. We wish to pay homage."

The child remained quiet, his gaze remaining fixed upon me, the silent companion of the man who was asking him questions. His mind focused on his mother, who was dying from a terrible strain of the bubonic plague, and then fluttered to his stomach and how he would feed his family and sickly matriarch.

"He's hungry … and afraid," I said, pointing out what Mordecai was unable to see, apparently having lost the gift to read minds with his lack of feeding from healthy blood. "His mother is sick, as well. Perhaps if we helped him, he would help us."

Mordecai looked up at me, his pale skin shining in the moonlight as he studied my face. He bit his lip and nodded, returning his gaze to the boy, who stood there in shock. His mind became abuzz with questions as to how I knew about his mother and the problems he faced. I smiled at the child, the kind of fake smile you do when dealing with a person you don't like.

"If you help my mum, I'll tell you where our lord stays on nights like these," he said, his voice weakened from hunger. His yellow eyes shimmered in the light of the moon, awaiting our answer to his proposition. I nodded to Mordecai, and sent him images of bread soaked with my blood. He shook his head at me, protesting their fate as ghouls or servants to us.

"I will not feed before soaking the bread. His mother will eat the bread, become cured of her plague, and will never become a ghoul, for that is a worse fate than dying of this despicable plague. She will grow old and get to see her children live and prosper," I whispered to Mordecai, appealing to his humanity.

Mordecai released a heavy sigh, thinking about the terrible effects that may occur if the sick mother ate the bloodied bread. He began to pray that I kept my word, but he eventually agreed to the plan that I had devised.

"If we feed you and your family, and cure your mother, will you tell us where your lord lives?" Mordecai asked the child, who immediately began nodding after he heard the part about his mother.

He instructed us to follow him, leading us into a small shanty that housed the dying beast that was his mother. Sweat glistened upon her skin as the torches embraced her in their smoky light. She moaned in pain as we gazed upon her blackened and swollen lymph nodes.

A crimson tear came across Mordecai's face as he felt the pain she was enduring, but only a smile crawled across my face. I handed the boy a few coins to buy bread and food for his family. I told him to quickly come back to the shanty as fast as his small legs could carry him. He nodded, understanding the faster he accomplished his task the quicker his mother would be cured.

The child danced through the door of the shanty with food filling his arms and pockets. He presented to me a small loaf of bread, still warm from the baker's oven. I smiled at him with approval as I told him to wait outside until we called him back, not wanting him to know what or how his mother became cured.

He left unwillingly, putting up a fierce fight to stay and ensure his mother was not harmed. Mordecai embraced the child in his arms, consoling him and promising no harm would fall to his mother as long as my blue-eyed companion breathed. The child left reluctantly after that, poking his head in every so often to see what the two strangers he brought home were doing.

"When did you last feed, Asael? That boy does not deserve to lose a mother to a vampire, nor does this lovely woman deserve to become a ghoul," Mordecai said. His eyes studied me as he waited for my response.

"I haven't fed since last night. The blood has worked through my system, and this pathetic creature will not be harmed," I said, grabbing the bread from its resting place.

I brought my claws to my fleshy wrist, digging into the soft flesh as I dragged down. Dark crimson nectar bubbled to the surface, spilling onto the bread and softening the crust, changing the white soft flesh of the bread into a soggy red. My eyes glistened as the euphoric pain rippled through my system, a smile dancing across my face.

I nodded to Mordecai, who took the bread over to the sweaty creature who was the child's mother. He gently placed the bloody bread into her mouth, and whispered "chew" into her ear. He carefully brought his hand up to her jaw, gently helping her chew the bread that lay within her cavernous mouth.

Her body convulsed violently as the dark nectar pulsated through her system, the vampiric blood breaking her free from the icy talons of death. The eyes of the creature popped open, her gray orbs gazing upon the two messiahs who had saved her from eternal damnation. A clammy claw beckoned her child, who was waiting in the doorway, peering in to see how his matriarch was.

He ran to her, calling her name as he advanced toward her bedside. Tears flowed from his cheek as his mother embraced him in her arms, kisses on the cheek and lips exchanged between the two infernal beasts of humanity. A smile came across Mordecai's face as he witnessed the act of unwavering love, a dark red tear streaming down his face.

A smile even crossed my own face, but not for the same reason that Mordecai was smiling. My smile was much more insidious than Mordecai; my smile was filled with the glorious truth that these two would never be humans again. My blood would strengthen them, make them faster, and more cunning, and with that, a new breed of humans would rise. But I digress; they shall come later in our story.

With his mother cured and their bellies filled, the child spilled all he knew about the lord of the town, including where he lived. This devious creature that held nobility in the eyes of the humans lived upon a hill, encased in massive walls and surrounded by legions of soldiers. My mouth salivated at the thought of bloody rivers flowing down into the village.

"I'll end the tyranny of the lord, and when I return, we shall take the riches to the peasants who need them the most," I said, making sure I understood the plan fully.

Mordecai nodded, a smile still plastered to his pale face. We departed each other's company, each one having a different task before them, each one having an equally difficult obstacle. Mordecai went to the dirty slums that housed the peasants, and he would inform those most worthy that salvation was coming to them, and that their God had heard their prayers.

Me, the beast who loved to inflict pain upon their species, ironically had become the answer to those prayers. While Mordecai was preaching to the filth of the countryside, it was my task to slaughter the tyrant who held their lives in his dirty claws. The darkness of night covered my stealthy ascension from the domain of the dirty to that of the wicked.

As I found my way to the palatial fortress that housed the blue-blooded tyrant, anger swam within my throat. What was supposed to be a fun and simple task quickly evolved into a painful ordeal. I found myself clawing my way upward, ascending the stone walls of the infernal citadel that harbored my prey. Though difficult work, it allowed my mind to focus on the delectable task I had, and I found solace in the great taste and warmth this blue-blooded lord would garner me.

After what felt like centuries, I stood on the top of his barrier, gazing upon the beauty of the night from a viewpoint I never experienced. The ants of humanity danced and twirled as they prepared for bed. Soon there would be one less among the infestation. I quickly scrambled down the wall, descending far faster than my previous climb upward. When my feet finally rested upon the dirt ground, images of death and slaughter danced within my body. The parasitic cretin who fed from the death and disease of the pathetic peasants would soon be nothing but a drained husk.

"Come out, come out wherever you are," I whispered as I breached the walls of the castle.

Chapter Six

The warmth of the building danced around me and embraced me like a motherly hug. Mosaics and murals lined the walls and tapestries and exotic rugs covered the floor. The sound of silence filled the halls of the stone structure, the quiet sound of my steps breaking its presence as I walked the premises. Sweet smells and odors poured from every angle, and the further I progressed the stronger they assaulted my senses. Dim firelight illuminated the passages as I navigated closer and closer to what I hoped was the resting place of the tyrannical bastard.

"Excuse me, sir?" a voice echoed.

I turned slowly, gazing upon a fair-skinned maiden holding a tray of various drinks and meats. Her hazel eyes studied me with fear, not knowing the male intruder who was now walking their halls. Her lower lip quivered as I stared at her, but I only smiled as I advanced toward her, my hand outstretched to hold hers.

The soft flesh of her hand entered mine, and squeezing it gently, I brought it to my lips and kissed it softly. The sweet taste of perfume rested on my lips as my eyes met hers, the delicate hazel reflecting in the torchlight, shimmering like tidal pools near the coast. She smiled, showing perfect white teeth and healthy gums, and when I saw this, the dark voices informed me that she was the daughter of the lord, and she was bringing him food and drink after his nightly ritual of having his way with the other maidens.

"May I ask what you are doing in my father's home?" she asked timidly.

"I simply came to pay homage to him. Inform him of news that is of a most pressing matter. Would you please tell me where I could find him?" I lied.

The human female, unknown to the greatness of guile, allowed me to pass into the realm of her father's domain. As I bowed before the girl, showing my gratitude, I began to sniff out the lord of this realm, the pheromones that exuded from him filling my nostrils as I walked to him swiftly and gracefully, my feet barely making a sound as I found my way to the master's room.

Blocking my entrance, however, was a massive wooden door. I can remember a smile embracing my lips as I marveled at the heavy object that sealed the room. My claws rose to touch the surface, feeling the smooth grain as I slid my hand downward, caressing the work done to the wood. My mind became filled with regret as my arm tore through the door, breaking it into splinters as I entered the den of a vile beast.

Even more extravagant linens and silks adorned the walls of this latest chamber. Bright reds and blues danced into my eyes as I gazed around the room, scanning for my potential prey. Among the various bodies within the room was a very angry German lord, his enraged obscenities becoming muffled by the swooning and screams of the wonderfully naked maidens that filled his chamber.

My pupils must have swelled into the glowing violet gems that expose my bestial nature, for the angry lord immediately dropped to his knees once he gazed upon them. He groveled and begged for a second chance as I walked closer to him, my lips contorted to a devilish grin that could only grow larger.

"Dear God, who art in heaven … please protect me from this demon," said the Lord, his hands making the cross as I lurched toward him, my hands grabbing his collar and hoisting him up into the air like a ragdoll.

"No amount of prayers can save you now, my lord. Your sins, which are numerous, blot your soul like dirt on a soiled rag. The indulgences that you bought recently shall be put to the test, though I doubt God favors the rich and privileged," I said as I brought him closer to my lips.

His heartbeat began to race as he peered into my mouth, seeing my canine teeth grow into more dominant fangs. I brought his pale, fleshy neck to my lips, and with the vampiric greed that I always loved, I drank from the blue-blooded tyrant with great joy. His blood sent chills down my spine, its pristine nectar untouched by the dirty diseases that the disgusting peasants endured day in and day out.

Once his body became nothing but a dry husk, I threw him away with great gusto, his limbs dancing in the air as he sailed across the room. His skull made a wonderful cracking sound as it hit the stone wall, and at that I smiled, only to realize, however, the maidens did not appreciate it as I did.

They were silent, but not in fear, rather in awe. Their minds sang out in wonder as they observed what I had done and how easy it had been. Their maniacal master's reign had ended, and by a benevolent stranger who would do them no harm, and ask for no gifts of the flesh for rescuing them from their bondage.

"Where did your lord keep his coins and money?" I asked, using their awe to speed my task along its way now that the fun part was over.

Their mouths moved but only silence walked out of them. Their naked skin, which was creamy and soft to the touch, became infested with goose bumps as they gazed upon the creature that had burst through the wooden door and killed their master. Their minds never moved away from my image and what I was. They were ghouls of a completely different kind.

They advanced forward, circling around to study me further. The sound of giggles and the sensation of prodding cascaded around me, and I felt my face beginning to snarl as my patience for the lovely maidens evaporated quickly. One moved in closer, resting her hand on my bicep and gazing into my eyes, which by now had changed back into their original obsidian color.

Her thoughts danced from what I was and what I had done to the riches that the tyrant horded. She silently nodded to me as she beckoned the others to back away and allow me to leave. They danced away from me in unison, giggling like children as they followed the unspoken command that emanated from their leader, and then lined up along the stone wall that was directly behind me.

The leader came close again, and brought her soft pink lips up to my ear. Without waiting for me to react to this strange scene, she whispered quietly into my ear, "What you seek lies within the darkness of the catacombs, among the festering corpses of long-deceased ancestors."

I nodded to the frail creature before me, who in turn led the other maidens out of the chamber, hastened footsteps spewing them out into the soulless halls, hoping to escape to freedom and join their human brethren once more.

The cold wind that whipped outside attacked the very fiber of my being as I stepped out into the darkness of the fiercely quiet night. The only audible sound was the howl of the vicious winds. I followed a beaten path that led to the catacombs, covered in idols and divine symbols that praised the false messiah that the German tyrant followed. I felt uneasy as I walked this routinely trodden path to the vault of the dead. Those who were once so zealous in their living years that they became celebrated in their rotting eternal slumber, their voices reverberating in my skull and their cold presence lingering in my heart.

My hand carefully pushed open the decaying door, the sweet scent of putrid flesh wafting into my nostrils as I descended into the hallowed caverns. Skulls and candles lined the narrow passageway as I stumbled around blindly, unaware of what dark surprises the tyrannical noble tucked away from the eyes of society, and the silent sound of echoing footsteps surrounded me. I progressed slowly, for though I knew the corpses were only corpses, I still harbored some superstitious beliefs about the dead rising, the only memories of my mortality being filled with this fear.

The air became thicker with the scents of death as I reached the bottom, finding myself in a well-lit mausoleum that was adorned with the bodies of the dead. The sight of them all was eerie, seeing the skeletal remains wearing the garb of the era, their mouths open agape. Their empty eyes stared off into the distance, making contact but at the same time avoiding my gaze. I had to shake off the chills that were washing over me, but each time I did that, the dead voices screeched in purgatorial limbo, and the chills would return stronger than before.

In the center of this monstrosity was a chair and table, flooded with gems and jewelry. On the chair sat the skeletal remains of a loved one, pieces of flesh still clinging to her weakening bones, a lovely lace dress covering her and jewels adorning what small amount of sickening green skin she retained. Her lips, parted and dangling from the strings of flesh that attached them to her mouth, was covered with a vibrant red substance that made them irresistibly enticing, and if she were alive, she would have been the talk of the town. Placed within her dainty hand were notes and letters of various lengths, confessing the mysterious writers undying love for the lady, yearning for her to come back and live forever in body as well as spirit, the crazed confessions of a sad soul.

Her skin, though decayed and rotting, was still soft to the touch, and if one searched for an unblemished oasis on her skin, one could tell that she had a fair complexion. A quick scan of my surroundings, and the dead voices singing praises of unbelievable love, told me that this corpse in front of me was that of the lord's favorite mistress or wife, which one I was never quite certain. The darkened voices spoke in reverence of the beautiful human who once inhabited the bones and flesh that lay before me. They spoke of her kindness and benevolence, how no matter what station in life you inhabited, she always accepted you, and tried her very best to make you feel welcome.

The voices spoke further, but no longer about her deeds during her waking years, instead revolving around her death. Shallow whispers and harmonious conversations all crept along the walls of society at her disappearance, and many conspiracies were born about her absence. The villagers, seeing the brutality and madness that their lord showed them, accused him of murder, noting that the madness started days after her disappearance, claiming she was but a stepping-stone into the oceans of insanity. The voices crawled further into my mind, shedding light upon the sad truth.

She died of this terrible plague that gripped the countryside in its icy fist. She grew weaker and weaker by the day, and when the inky black blotches covered her skin, she committed suicide in her bedroom. The note, among those held firmly in her hand, spoke of eternal peace and salvation from the demonic plague that embraced her.

I'll admit, when I discovered who the decaying corpse was that lay in front of me, a tear came to my eye, for the lord I killed was not the malevolent demon that the lowly dirt-encrusted pieces of filth thought he was, nor was he that tyrannical bastard I saw him as. He was just a grief-stricken husband, mourning the passing of a loved one he adored fervently. It was with great remorse and regret that I took the jewels from the dead corpse, knowing that the person I should've cured was the blue-blooded lord I sent to oblivion mere moments ago, my only consolation being he suffered no longer.

When I stepped out of the catacombs, I could feel the anger and woe rising within my throat, growing with each passing step. The darkened voices, still praising the dead woman, filled my ears as I made my way toward the stone walls that imprisoned me temporarily in the courtyard of the dead hermit lord. My claws scraped across the rock surface as I propelled upward, eventually lifting myself onto the top of the wall that protected a dead madman. The original awe of the countryside at my current angle did not return, and instead was replaced with anger for the vermin who filled the landscape before me.

They would all pay in due time, but sadly I would have no part in their retribution.

I eventually found myself outside the lair that had housed our presence through this vile era. I found my blue-eyed companion within its rotting walls. Those blue eyes became filled with idiotic glee when he saw the jewels and treasures I brought back with me, and I noticed a bloody tear danced down his cheek. His mind sang out with images of salvation and healing for the filthy parasites who were his peasant friends, and the sensation of disgust filled my stomach.

"You know the lord you had me kill was not a tyrant," I said, my voice emotionless and calm as I stared at the wall.

"He was a power-hungry sycophant who preyed off of the weak," Mordecai responded angrily.

"No, he was a depressed, grieving husband who fell into madness when the love of his life was carried away from the exact plague she fought so valiantly to eradicate. He became a hermit, and did not care for the problems of his realm anymore. His life, in his mind, was not worth living without the lady that death took before her time," I said with a snarky tone, correcting Mordecai's false statement.

He said nothing, and his mind lay silent. He cared little for the upper class noble who had to die so that others could live. In his mind, one life was a just price for hundreds of lives to be saved, and while he was right, this one life we took did not deserve to be taken.

His claws caressed the jewelry, the cool sensation of metal sending shivers across his body. His mind flared with the thoughts of appreciation he would receive from those he cared for most of all in this cruel world. He immediately set out to do what he thought needed to be done for his missionary work.

When I awoke the next night, he was nowhere to be seen.

Chapter Seven
Mordecai's Madness

Mordecai was gone, off gallivanting with the peasants and dishing out the treasures of the previous night's raid. My stomach churned from the guilt of killing the lord. It was a long lost sensation to me. Because of this I could not bring myself to feed from the blood-soaked meat puppets that surrounded me. I remained within the confines of our sacred hideout, brooding from the enlightening encounter I had experienced earlier.

Hours passed, and when I finally summoned the will to vacate the stone walls of the church, a frightened knock echoed from the door. The knocks continued, and then I heard the sobbing of a young man. Fearing the worst, I opened the door quickly, and saw on the doorstep a hunched over Mordecai, blood staining his clothing and face as he cried furiously.

"Mordecai?"

He responded with a nod, tears streaming from his beautiful blue eyes.

"What is wrong, my friend? I haven't seen you cry like this since you created that ghoul."

He wiped away his crimson tears with a dirty claw covered in rosary beads, and after a few minutes composed himself to speak. He tried his best to compose himself, and then looked me in the eyes, his pupils dilated from indulging in a delicacy that was despised by him: the blood of humans.

"The peasants were overjoyed at the sight of the treasure," he began. "They praised me and hugged me, and we drank in celebration. The delicious mortal nectar that is alcohol swam down my gullet smoothly and without resistance, and after a few flagons of the honey wine, I was not myself anymore. The drink went to my head, Asael.

"I changed completely, no longer caring for the weak and the downtrodden. Anger clouded every judgment I made, loathing and hatred filled every word I spoke. It was terrifying. It took all of my patience and energy to not maim and maul the peasants that surrounded me, and thankfully when the vile drink was gone their celebration ended, leaving me alone and filled with the putrid emotions that no doubt infect you each and every miserable day.

"The terrible beast within me wanted blood, yearned for it like a starving child yearns for the scraps of the aristocrats. My throat burned, my veins ached, and I knew that if I did not do something quickly, I would give in to this vile beast that I had become. I allowed my instincts to take over, though I regret doing so, and followed my feet to the doors of the only church in the whole town.

"Inside, the candles burned brightly, illuminating the wooden walls and stained pews with their orange hue, the scent of sacramental wine saturating the air. My head was swimming with contempt for the weakness that divine obedience gives the peasants, and the sight of the priest that inhabited the church sent me into a blood frenzy.

"The elderly holy man never saw me, but I remember his heartbeat rising dramatically when he heard my demonic laughter echoing through his sacred walls. I pounced upon him, pinning him on the ground and revealing the sight of the wrinkled neck that would quiet the infernal beast that danced within my head. The blood began to gush into my mouth as I pierced the flesh of his neck.

"I actually smiled at the despicable feeling that I was experiencing, loving every minute of it."

His hands shook as the memories of what he had done flooded his mind, the dark images of brutality plaguing the shadowed alleys of his memory. Tears began to well up in his eyes, but they dried as soon as they appeared. With a heavy sigh, my companion continued his tale of that night.

"The priest lay there, the last breaths of his short life filled with agony, and I stared at him with bestial glee as I knew I was the cause of his terrible suffering. The beast that I was took great pleasure in his torment, relishing every last moment of the sad end to the great miracle that was his life. When he was finished struggling, my hands stripped his cooling body of his clothing and placed it upon my warming skin, making the wolf that killed the shepherd the newest shepherd of sheep.

"It didn't end there, however. Killing one man was not enough to fill the dark void. The creature that clutched my heart sapped my vitality as soon as it came to me. It demanded that I feed again, only promising to stop once it was appeased. I walked into the cool nighttime streets, the scent of wine and sight of candles abandoning me as I ventured further and further away from the church and closer and closer to an orphanage that was down the street from the church. A sickening smile crossed my face, Asael, as I entered the large structure that the young humans begrudgingly called their home.

"They were excited to see me, the poor innocent youths, grasping at the stolen rosary and gasping at the new priest who had come to visit the lambs of his flock. Their smiles and innocence will forever be scrawled in my mind, my friend, and never again will I be able to live with myself the same.

"They asked, some even begged, for confession, demanding to be alone with the new stranger who came into their world, completely trusting the brand new face who stalked their lives. My dark half was delighted to hear their request, and made sure to please them as fast as he possibly could. We found an empty room, and each child marched in with great gusto and glee. They marched in like cattle, unknowingly awaiting their slaughter."

He bit his lip and didn't say anything, the disturbing images of the broken children filling the expanses of his mind. His jaw began to shake as the images assaulted him, and tears flowed freely down his pale cheeks as he looked into my unusually sympathetic eyes. While I despised humanity, seeing my companion vulnerable and weakened to tears was something my cold heart couldn't take, and if it weren't for years of anger and rage, I may have wept with my friend.

"One of the children, a sweet and delicate flower whose name escaped the hideous cretin that inhabited my mind, sat right upon my lap and looked up at me with eyes full of wonder. She smiled widely at me, even gave me a soft hug, and thanked me for offering her confession. Her frail frame and weak voice, accompanied by her gentle manner, made me weep inside my imprisoned mind," he said.

"What is your sin, my child?" he had asked her, trying best to mimic the priests at the various churches we frequented.

"I stole some bread, Father. The orphanage ran out of food for a slight period of time, and my brother kept giving me his food so I wouldn't feel hunger," she said, sobbing.

"Come to me, my child, embrace me one last time, and in the eyes of God you shall be forgiven," he told her, allowing her tiny fragile arms to wrap around his neck.

Her soft, pale neck shone in the candlelight, and the creature that Mordecai had become grinned wickedly as his teeth sank forcefully into the youthful veins of his prey. She screamed in pain, tears welling up in her eyes quickly as the sensation shot outward. Her mouth became locked into the terrifying expression that wiped across her face as the essence of her life drained slowly like a sieve into my companion's mouth, her death providing strength and power to his eternal life.

"Her blood was the very embodiment of innocence. I could see all her memories and dreams within the scarlet poison that crept down my throat, and though the devil that I had become relished the images, a dark red tear slithered down my putrid cheek.

"The monster that possessed my body and mind discarded the sweet angel as if she were a broken doll, allowing her body to be hidden behind my own. I requested the next child to enter, my thirst for blood and the yearning to feel normal overpowering any darkness plaguing my mind. I did not care who my victim was, Asael, I just wanted to inflict the same feeling that I endured day in and day out for centuries. I wanted them to know what it felt like to hate the very thing you are," he said, staring into my eyes.

"The door quietly opened, and from behind the threshold popped a raven-haired child with fair skin, sapphire eyes, and a carefree smile. She danced toward me, her soft hair jumping to and fro, her quiet giggle filling the small room."

"Hello, Father, how are you today?" she asked innocently with a smile, her teeth catching the burning torchlight.

"Very well, my dear, very well indeed. Why don't we get business out of the way, and confess to me, my child?" Mordecai said, his hand gently patting her shoulder.

"She looked up at me, her eyes brimming with tears as her sins came to the forefront of her mind, her sapphire gems shimmering in the orange torchlight. Her lip quivered as she thought of the impure deeds that she had committed in the name of survival, the sins of the flesh she was forced to endure in order to live just one more day. She buried her head in my chest, her tears flowing freely, soaking the black linen of my priestly trappings," said Mordecai, his voice saturated with regret as his memories erupted from his mouth.

"The headmaster of the orphanage plays with me in his room, and if I'm a good girl and does everything he says, he gives me extra rations," she said, her tears forging rivers among banks of caked-on dirt.

"And is it safe for me to assume that you eat these rations he gives you?" asked Mordecai, patting her on the back to try to console her from crying.

"She shook her head 'no,' her hand rising to wipe away the streams of tears that danced across her face. She huffed and puffed, waved her hand to indicate to me to come closer, and when my ear was to her lips, she muttered the words that weaken me dearly when I think of them," said the blue-eyed vampire with great remorse.

"I give the extra rations to the younger orphans," she confessed, her blue eyes twinkling as the words raced from her lips and into my pale companion's ears, sending the dark beast within Mordecai shuddering at the thought of human compassion and love.

"The creature within me weakened and lost his control quickly. I craved her blood more than any of the children who dwelled within the orphanage. My lips quaked with desire, the sticky claws of the infernal beast clutching my mind, yearning to tear into her, and I could no longer resist the bloody temptation that bubbled within me.

"I brought my hand to her head, petting her black hair gently at first, lulling her into a false sense of security and understanding. She melted in my hand, her body falling limp and peaceful on my lap. I'll admit, Asael, a sadistic smile scurried across my face as I dug my other hand into her chest, my nails ripping and cutting the soft flesh that encased the bone and organs that made up the frail child.

"She screamed in pain, the kind of blood-churning scream that makes courageous men stand still and do nothing. My other hand gripped her mouth, causing the lips to contort and mash together, muffling her screams with delightful satisfaction. Her arms flailed and her hands bombarded my sides as she tried to escape my powerful grip.

"Blood poured quickly from her chest wound, and her speed and strength slowly sapped away as the crimson liquid that you love so much poured from the gaping hole, covering the floor with its velvety texture," explained Mordecai, his words awakening great excitement within me.

"And then … when I finally saw what I had done, the pain and death I had wrought, the dark creature left. No longer did his greasy claws cling to my fragile mind; no longer did the darkness of the dead crawl within my heart. I was freed from the terrible fate that plagued me, but at the same time, I was imprisoned with the guilt that flooded my heart from the horrendous actions I had committed," said Mordecai, his voice returning to the characteristically sad tone he always had throughout his life.

"Mordecai, your actions on that night were not your fault. You said it yourself; the demonic presence of alcohol possessed you tonight," I said, attempting to make my eternal friend feel better.

He moved away from me quickly, guilt gnawing at his heart as the voices of his victims rang in his ears. The slimy claws of the dark beast that clouded his mind still lingered within him, for alcohol does not leave our dormant system easily, and so I had to choose my words carefully, for I knew Mordecai did not wish to become an insidious parasite once more.

He stared at me, crimson tears welling up in front of his cobalt eyes as he gazed into mine for what seemed like hours, completely bathed in the sweet silence of a creature deep in thought. He stirred every so often, tilting his head one way or the other, his mind racing with the thoughts of a grief-stricken man.

"How do you do it, Asael?" asked Mordecai, breaking the delicate silence that I had been enjoying.

"You've asked this question before, my friend," I replied quickly, dodging the question the best I could.

"No, how do you live? How do you not care that we are beasts among men? That we are tumors upon society, parasites of humanity?" asked Mordecai, once again returning to the usual ploy of trying to change me when he became filled with grief and guilt.

I didn't answer right away. I just sat there, glaring at the pathetic creature who lay in front of me. My mind flared with the images and voices of my victims, their death only occurring to help me provide sustenance for my own life. Mordecai knew that I enjoyed being what I was, and because he loathed his existence, he demanded I remain as guilt filled and miserable as he was.

"You ask me how I live. You ask me how is it that I can feed every night, taste the crimson blood that flows from our prey like a river, and not feel an ounce of guilt. These questions have been asked before.

"Tonight, you saw and felt what I see and feel each night. The darkness clouds your mind and you just act. Instinct washes over you and your actions are guided by an animalistic urge. Its one aim is to survive and receive pleasure or sustenance," I said, impatience dripping from my words.

"Yet I hated every minute of it," Mordecai said quickly, trying to poke holes in my argument.

"Did you? You said yourself that it felt good to give out the same amount of pain that you feel day in and day out. Deep down, Mordecai, we all enjoy our animal instincts; just some of us can't stomach giving into them every day," I said, gripping Mordecai's shoulder tightly.

"Perhaps humanity only needs one Morning Star, Asael." said Mordecai with a slight smile.

"And for every devil, there shall be an angel," I replied, smiling back at my friend.

Chapter Eight

The nights that followed Mordecai's insidious bloodbath at the orphanage passed us by, and we both felt terror in our hearts. Humanity, after centuries of playing defense, had switched their position to a vengeful offense. They hired a vampire hunter. The church, its festering claws clutching everything it could, found the diabolical cretin dwelling in a crypt. They would attempt to destroy us, hoping to gain retribution from our destruction.

The putrid creature slithered among human society like the serpent he was. His scent was that of rotting flesh and bitter ale, driving normal folk away from him at all costs, and the few words he did speak were saturated with anger. The priests themselves barely tolerated his diabolical presence, despising the sight of the pale-faced bastard who reminded them of the demons who stalked their nightmares.

The clergy banished the vile creature from their sacred grounds as soon as possible, sending him on his way to do the work at hand. His boots clicked against the stone as he stalked the midnight streets of the hushed town, scanning through every dark alleyway for the festering creature that destroyed the orphanage.

"Come out, come out, wherever you are," he would occasionally sing, his hoarse voice echoing against the brick structures around him.

His search danced into the night as he effortlessly awaited the inevitable attack that would descend upon the flock of sheep that were the peasants he was paid to protect. And finally, after carefully waiting, his lovely piece of bait slithered into view.

The small, frail child shivered in the cool night air as she panhandled for food and coins to help sustain her miserable existence. Her pale face was covered in grime and dirt; she resembled a pathetic prisoner with her emaciated frame and short stature. Her brown eyes, dim and unimpressive, stared at anything that passed by with a glazed, uninterested glare. When the Hunter approached, she attempted to scurry away from him, afraid of the unknown entity who approached her, but fatigue and weakness forced her to stay in her place and speak to the beast at her feet.

"Hello, darling," he said hoarsely, the words muffled behind the scarf covering his mouth. "How are you this fine evening?"

"Good," she said sheepishly, terrified of what the monster in men's clothing might want.

"Are you hungry, my dear?" he asked her, his gloved hand reaching into the black leather satchel hanging down by his side, grabbing a warm loaf of bread.

The little girl's eyes burned brightly at the magnificent sight of bread, and her head bobbed up and down slowly, indicating a yes. Her small, fragile hands shot out from her chest and ripped the bread from the vampire hunter's hands, tearing the soft bread into chunks and placing them delicately in her mouth, relishing the soft texture.

"Thank you, sir," the child said once she had started the wonderful work of finishing the bread.

"Anything for a dear, sweet child such as you," said the Hunter as he placed his gloved hand upon her head, gently rubbing her hair.

The night waned as he sat next to the child, watching her shiver and shake until finally the delicate embrace of slumber blanketed her small body. His eyes gleamed as he watched the peaceful angel drift away into dreams of a life full of food and comfort, and the thought of the struggles the fragile child faced every day brought a single, cloudy tear to the Hunter's eye.

An hour had passed since the child had fallen asleep when the Hunter finally decided to leave her. His mind was clouded with the thoughts and voices of the children who had become tainted by the demons that attacked them. He yearned for justice and vengeance. His heart burned for the blood of the creatures that harmed the angels, and he would not rest until their demise was realized.

Like his mind, his feet wandered as well, carrying him through the various streets that snaked around buildings and dwellings, and it was during this mindless journey through the streets that he finally came upon Mordecai, who had been feasting from a rather fat cat. The creature squirmed in Mordecai's hands, the blood pouring from the veins of the animal into his mouth, giving him the strength he needed to survive.

"Evening, Mordecai," said the Hunter, his eyes gazing upon the pale flesh of the blue-eyed vampire.

Mordecai, blood dripping from his mouth, stared at the creature in front of him in awe. The Hunter, covered in head to toe in a black cloak with a wide-brimmed hat and black gloves, returned the stare. His clouded black eyes bored holes into the blue gems of Mordecai as he came closer.

"Evening, stranger," replied Mordecai, wiping the blood from his lips.

"Oh, come now, do you not recognize your own brother?" asked the Hunter, lowering the coif that covered his face, revealing a festering, decayed necrotic jaw and fanged grin.

"I'm afraid I'm terrible with faces," replied Mordecai, stepping away from the ghastly sight of the Hunter's face.

"You don't know how truly lucky you are, Mordecai. The dark voices ceased to crawl within your mind, and never again did you have to deal with their incessant chanting in your mind, hearing their words slither within yourself, knocking on the inside of your skull," he said, advancing toward Mordecai with great haste, grabbing the blue-eyed vampire by the collar and trapping him in place.

"Ephraim?!" replied Mordecai incredulously

"In the flesh," he said with a sadistic smile.

"But … how? I saw your body turn to ash when Cain drank your blood," said Mordecai.

"As you can see, I do not dwell within my skin. Like a demon, I possess the trappings of a mortal, using his dead flesh as a meat puppet to affect the mortal realm," Ephraim said coldly.

"How is that even possible?" Mordecai exclaimed.

"There are things that no mortal, or immortal, should ever know. The voices still spoke to my weakened spirit in the realm of the dead, informing me that I could be reborn if I could only find a vacant corpse that no spirit clung to.

"When this ancient trick danced across my ears, I began to scour the realm, wading through lakes of fire and rivers of acid to try and find such a body. The decayed husk that I now dwell within, the only shell with no tormented soul lurking in it, had once belonged to a pious priest who preached to the sheep that dwell on these pitiful streets, the same sheep whose orphans you fed from," he said with a slight snap to his voice.

Mordecai edged his way backward, attempting to place distance from the beast in human skins, his feet carefully and gracefully moving him further and further into the dark alley that he haunted.

"Ephraim, I promise you I felt terrible about what happened. I thought Cain was unjust in what he had done to you, and had I been as strong as I am now, I would've stopped him," said Mordecai, attempting to console the predator who stalked him further into the dead-end dark alley that harbored them both.

"You could have stopped him. You were practically his equal," snapped Ephraim, anger fueling the decayed husk's flame of hatred.

The claws of the necrotic nuisance snapped out, gripping Mordecai's neck with the undead strength of an ancient vampire, dragging my blue-eyed friend up to his face. The stench of Ephraim's breath wafted into Mordecai's nostrils, making my companion gag as the scent of rotting flesh and bitter ale assaulted his senses. The eyes of Ephraim, clouded and black, stared into Mordecai's, his obsidian orbs filled with hatred and loathing. They studied the perfect canvas that was Mordecai's features, and they betrayed their master's intent.

"You can't kill him, Ephraim," said Mordecai with a wicked smile, realizing the Hunter's real purpose.

Ephraim glared into Mordecai's sapphire eyes, his rage replaced with confusion and curiosity.

"Why is that, Mordecai?" inquired Ephraim.

A slight chuckle erupted from Mordecai's mouth, which was followed by a wickedly satisfied grin. My blue-eyed companion brought his lips up to the Hunter's ear, and with great satisfaction, confessed to Ephraim the numerous reasons why his task was futile.

"Unlike you, who became insane after dealing with the voices, the one you seek has managed to embrace his curse, and even embrace the dark voices that dance within his skull. You were doomed the moment you agreed to help destroy us. Satan himself will pity your pathetic soul when it returns to his realm, the horrendous torture known to the one you seek surpassing none," said Mordecai, his smile unwavering.

Ephraim released Mordecai once the words left his lips. The young fledgling he once knew had grown into a completely different breed of demonic parasite that he never would have expected myself to become, the blood of Cain acting as a catalyst for the darkness to grip onto and speed my evolution into a hellacious beast all that much quicker.

"He's shown no signs of madness?" asked Ephraim, all desire to kill being replaced by the curiosity as to why he was too weak to work through the pain he endured.

"None. Asael is the vampire that Cain should have been," said Mordecai with an even bigger smile, pride filling his voice as he thought of the years we shared .

Ephraim backed away slowly from his brother, the name of his murderer sending chills down his rotting spine. A reddish brown tear rolled down the Hunter's cheek as the memory of his death rushed into his mind, the dark voices singing in his ears of the power that his blood gave to Cain, only to have it ripped from him by myself..

"But wait … you also drank from Cain. Why are you not like Asael?" asked Ephraim.

"I am weak, and I loathe my existence. I feed only when I have to, and because of that, it leaves me vulnerable and frail," responded Mordecai.

"Like the humans you love so much," I replied, walking into the darkness of the alley.

Ephraim nearly jumped out of his corpse when he saw me walk from out of the shadows, fear covering his mind like a blanket. His hands, festering and filled with maggots, began to shake and tremble as I edged my way toward him, his black eyes drowning in bloody tears as I smiled at him. Every step I took forward, Ephraim took two steps backward, our boots creating a wonderful melody of terror and delight.

"What's wrong, Ephraim? Is the terrifying vampire hunter, who has become a reckless butcher for the church, afraid of two younger vampires?" I said, in a taunting voice.

"I'm not so foolish to assume the destroyer of our father is not stronger than I," replied Ephraim, his stare avoiding my own at all costs, as if staring into my eyes would turn him to stone.

"Don't worry, it'll be a quick death," sneered Mordecai.

Ephraim nodded as he heard Mordecai's fluttering words, but the Hunter's mind focused on the thought of Cain and the destruction and chaos that I alone had committed over the many years of my life. I smiled as my work plagued Ephraim's mind, like a child smiles as the ants underneath his magnifying glass combust into flame. It was wonderful to watch his face contort, showing disgust and dismay in wondrous displays.

The Hunter's body quaked as the images refused to leave his mind, the dark voices singing of my deeds with intense vigor and purpose, their immortal words never leaving Ephraim alone. The Hunter's claws dug into his scalp as he attempted to remove the despicable things from his mind by force. I merely laughed as I heard his claws crunch into his thick skull, finding it impossible to break the supernatural shell that housed the dark voices from harm.

Crimson tears flowed from the crazed vampire as his mind succumbed to the dark madness that plagued him. His eyes, black as the night sky and flooded with sadness, peered into my eyes with the remorse of a child who made an honest mistake. His mouth moved to form the words "I am sorry," as he convulsed on the ground and allowed the insanity to wash over him.

"Can we do anything to help him?" asked Mordecai.

"The dark voices say we shouldn't help. They wish for him to return to the realm of the dead, and return the corpse he commandeered," I replied, turning away from the rotting corpse that was once our brother Ephraim. Mordecai quickly followed once the stench of death flew from the festering corpse.

Once we arrived at our hideout, Mordecai wanted to talk about what had happened, and I begrudgingly agreed. He poised himself upon a chair, and with curious eyes, stared into my own, which were filled with delight for the death of an enemy.

"Ephraim asked if the madness that touched him has ever

touched you," said Mordecai softly, trying his best to remain calm, and not be swept into the maelstrom that was his mind at the time.

"Did he?" I said playfully, examining my nails by the candlelight of our domain.

"You said blood keeps it at bay ... right?" inquired my companion, his cobalt eyes locked onto me.

"That's what I said," I replied, my answer being carried by a dead and cold voice.

"Don't toy with me, Asael, you owe me an honest answer," said Mordecai, emotion washing over his voice.

I sighed heavily as my friend pushed his questions further, twisting the knife that was our camaraderie into my heart. I felt compelled to answer, but I knew the reaction from Mordecai would not be a pleasing one, and in the end I would have to suffer the incessant sympathy that my companion exuded whenever we were discussing my immortal years and eternal life.

"You ask me if the madness that Ephraim endured has ever graced me with its presence," I said, trying to make sure I understood the question to its fullest. Mordecai responded with an enthusiastic nod, to which I replied with a heavy sigh.

"Mordecai, when we lay down to sleep, do you dream?" I asked.

"I want to talk about this, Asael. Don't change the subject," he replied, a twang of anger covering his words.

"Do you dream?" I asked angrily.

"Vampires, as far as I know, cannot dream," said Mordecai with a touch of impatience.

"Well, Ephraim and I did. Each and every day, we would dream. Our dreams would not bring us to the fields of Elysium or to a sunny beach, but instead to the realm of the dead.

"There we would be attacked by the pitiful souls we had fed from, who would assault us with questions. They'd beg us to know why we chose them, why God condemned them to die early. Ephraim loathed it," I explained.

"You mean you two had interacted?" asked Mordecai.

"Have been ever since he died. His voice crawls within my skull, as Nafretiti's does and Cain's did. Together we would stand in front of the Lake of Fire and deal with our victims, one at a time. They begged and pleaded for us to make it all better, to make the pain go away. Ephraim used to weep like a baby, apologizing to each and every soul we took.

"But eventually, even he stopped apologizing to our countless victims. We would stand there, in a lake of dead souls, surrounded by the cries and screams of the tortured dead, and we remained emotionless as they moaned for answers," I said, a lump welling in my throat as the nightmares flooded my memory.

Mordecai rose from his seat and crossed the room. His sapphire eyes clouded with red tears as he looked at me in sadness, his clawed hand clutching my shoulder with the grip of the dead. His lips contorted to a frown, and a small sigh passed his lips as his grip tightened. His head nodded, like a friend's does when they try to understand your tribulation.

"You'll never understand until you witness the experience. You'll never know what it's like to see Lucifer himself laughing at you as you wade in a sea of dead souls," I said solemnly, getting up from seat and leaving Mordecai in the room by himself.

Slumber would come, and nightmares would infest my mind once more.

Chapter Nine
The Nightmare

I awoke to find myself in a field of blood, grass, and scorched trees, the sound of chirping bats filling the air. My feet carried me to the bank of a river. Its waters ran black with the souls of the fallen. My fists clenched as I realized that I had returned to the bowels of the most insidious habitat of evil, and I would find no solace among its inhabitants.

The chirping of the bats was drowned out by the cracks of a whip and the screams of the impure bastards who were cursed to dwell within their prison of fire, bone, and blood. My head jerked around to try to capture the sound, only to have my eyes gaze upon the tormenter of the fallen creature. My heart sank deep within my chest.

The unholy beast who held the whip of bone had not changed since the last time I gazed upon him and his darkened spirit. His skin was still as black as my soul, his eyes still as white as milk. A sound erupted from his throat as he laughed and chortled at the sadistic pain he unleashed upon the chained parasite, his mind singing out in revenge when he thought of Mordecai and me. Cain had finally found his new God to follow; he found solace in the servitude of Satan.

His eyes discovered me, realizing he had a witness to the torture he was inflicting on the pathetic soul he had caught. His lips formed a smile, that sinister smile of a psychopathic sadist delving into his dark fetishes. Cain's vampiric lust was strengthened in hell, and no longer did he care for the children he sired and left on Earth. His paternal instinct had evaporated into the clouds of hatred that now stormed his mind. Our betrayal was the straw that broke the camel's back.

Cain's gaze remained locked on me, tracking me like a predator. He refused to utter any words to the abomination that sent him down to this dark domain.

"You've changed little, Father," I said, speaking first and putting the proverbial salt in an old wound.

"No longer am I your father," he spat. "I renounced the creature that God made, and have become a true servant to the darkness," he said proudly.

The anger that I had grown accustomed to all these centuries of living in the shadows gripped my mind and left me speechless, biting anger filling my heart and leaving me dumb.

Cain glared at me with smoldering rage, a slight chuckle escaping his throat as he nodded his head. His eyes studied me for a moment or two, his serpentine tongue licking his lips. His claws came up and rubbed his chin. He was deep in thought; his mind screaming out every dark and insidious thought about me that slithered into his demonic brain. I was poked and prodded like a piece of cattle, and my anger seethed when I realized that I had entered the domain of Cain, and I was powerless to stop him from doing anything to me in this realm. The power I gained from him was but a grain of sand in the desert of power he now possessed. The weak coward I had killed so long ago had trapped me, and he now became the powerful tyrant he always secretly wanted to be.

But when I thought the blade of pain would slice open my skin, sending shivers of agony to flow through my body, all I felt was an empty void of sensation. He stood there, powerless to do any real harm to me, as if I had been marked by some creature of vast power for protection. The more I pondered it, I realized exactly who would want to examine me, the very person I had been accused of being so many times in the past.

"Though I want to see your death, the Prince of Darkness refuses my wishes," admitted Cain.

He clutched my forearm and led me down an onyx pathway that brought us to a tall, black citadel that stood in front of a hideously bright sunset, the blood red ball of plasma setting right behind the Lake of Fire. The entire time, Cain was thinking about my body filleted and torn, pieces of me spiked upon shafts of metal to bake in the heat of the fire. This nightmare of mine had warped his personality and demeanor, though years later I would discover he changed very little.

Cain's claw pushed the rotted wooden door open, its hinges creaking from years of rust. Our feet clicked on the black marble floors as we advanced to the insidious throne room of hell, where I was to be introduced to the master of evil and the tempter of man.

Lying upon the throne of hell was a malnourished man, covered in a thin black cloak, the top of his face shrouded in shadows. He smiled at me, showing gnarled black teeth that contrasted with his pale skin. He pried himself from his thorny throne, limping slowly toward me. The closer he got to me, the stronger his scent became, the sweet stench of perfumed flowers and musk, a wondrous concoction to tempt any mortal.

"Welcome to hell, Asael," said the devil quietly.

I nodded in his direction, but no words came to my mind. The dark voices screamed in fear as the robed parasite crept closer to me, his grotesque, dirty claws stretching outward for a handshake. The voices told me to resist, but everything else inside me told me to embrace the beast who lay before me, for I knew eventually this mangled monster would demand my help, and I was filled with a yearning to have the fallen angel on my side.

My pristine hand clutched the filthy palm of Lucifer, and the voices of the dead in my mind fell quiet, whispering prophesies of my demise at the hand of the Morning Star. The devil smiled, his infernal fangs shining in the flames of the surrounding torches. His head began to shake slightly, comforting me knowing that my soul, if I had one, was not doomed to dwell here just yet.

"You are among friends, Asael. This nightmare of yours will soon be over, my child," he said.

"May I ask you a question that has plagued me for as long as I can remember?" I inquired respectfully.

He nodded, his smile fading to a stern face.

"Why is it that Ephraim and I dream, when no other vampire does?" I asked, studying the malnourished man as he was studying me.

The sickly, pale man laughed a booming roar as the question came from my mouth, the sound of which echoed throughout the cavernous domain of the stubborn angel. He smiled at me once more, his gnarled teeth piercing the veil that was his lips.

"You and Ephraim are not vampires in the same sense that Cain was and Mordecai is," he said. "Ephraim is plagued with madness, a disease of the mind. As we know, vampires are immune to disease of any kind, thus Ephraim was never a true vampire. In fact, he could enter the sunlight immediately, a feat that some ancients couldn't even do, the only result being his skin became a bit more radiant.

He was only a human who underwent the first death, but the curse never took full control of him."

"And myself? I, too, hear the voices of the dead, and I am subject to the infernal dreams that take me here each and every day," I said inquisitively with a tinge of anger.

Satan sighed heavily, and looked me square in the eyes. His smile returned, his white tongue licking his mangled teeth as his stare never wavering from my eyes. He moved in closer to me, his claws bracing my shoulders as his serpentine lips came closer to my ears.

"You are more than a vampire," he said with great enthusiasm. "Within your chest has grown the heart of a demon, a blood-drinking tyrant that knows no satisfaction.

"That night you killed Cain. It's all a blur, isn't it? The one night you can't truly remember. You think you do, but that is just a false memory fabricated to hide what happened, to repress the truth. When you awake, ask Mordecai what really happened that night, if he dares to bring the memories that haunted him for years back to the surface," said Lucifer.

I nodded to Lucifer, albeit confusedly, and I found my feet carrying me to the exterior of the monolithic mausoleum that was the black citadel housing the fallen angel. Things around me began to blur and lose focus as the nightmare I was experiencing began to slowly disappear, replaced with the familiar surroundings of an abandoned church.

I awoke from the nightmarish vision with the curiosity and intrigue of a child. My mind buzzed like a beehive with the questions that the Morning Star had placed there. My mind raced to find the first question that I would ask, and when I spotted my companion, the buzzing stopped and the race ceased.

"You look like you've seen the devil himself, Asael, is everything okay?" asked Mordecai, concerned.

My mouth opened, but the words wouldn't come out. I felt dumbstruck, finally understanding a little bit more of my curse fully, and realizing the power that I alone had at my disposal. Mordecai stared at me as my mouth opened and closed, trying to will the ability to speak my mind at this moment. Centuries of speaking, and now was the time that I forget how to utter syllables to form words and sentences.

"Do you remember the night Cain died?" I blurted out, the words dribbling from my mouth weakly.

His hands froze and his shoulders stiffened. His mouth hung agape and his eyes closed tightly, as if freezing in place would make the moment go away. He stayed there for a moment, frozen like a well-crafted statue of some kind, and then when he realized the question would not in fact flutter away, he relaxed and sat down, ready to tell the tale.

"Sadly, I can never forget that night. A strange feeling pulled at my heart, and I knew something terrible yet great would happen. You were flooded with anger about the torment you felt when it came to Ephraim's death, not wanting to feel compelled to mourn a stranger. My own anger clouded my judgment, and I pushed you into a problem you were unaware of, and together we sought revenge. We climbed the stairs that led to Cain's room. My mind was blank with fear, the constant nagging of the realization that our futures might never be the same. Your mind, however, was blazing with new hatred and rage, no second thoughts skirting across the surface. You felt as though you were chafing under the reign of Cain, and you demanded that he be put down like the dog that you thought he was. Your eyes were red with anger, draining the light from the torches surrounding us, and I saw that they were focused on the silhouette of our father.

"When he turned around to face us in his room, and a small

conversation ended, we attacked him to begin feeding from him. You immediately changed from an innocent fledgling into a dark demon bent on freedom, something I had never witnessed before or since, and it was that vile demon that swept Cain into the realm of the dead. I had stopped drinking—I only drank a mouthful of his blood. Disgust stopped me. But you demanded that I tasted the ancient blood that flowed like a fountain from our father's veins.

"A single tear fell from my eye as my lips embraced Cain's neck, and a symphony of insidious laughter flowed from you, crying out that I was weak, but the dark fluid would make me strong. The knowledge you gained from Cain made you the elder and me the fledgling, and that's how it has been ever since," explained Mordecai.

When Mordecai finished his tale, laughter embraced my mind, its slimy claws gripping tightly around it. It was a dark and satanic laughter, the kind that belonged to an ancient beast that would plague mankind with his nefarious plots for centuries to come. The laughter grew and grew until it no longer remained within my mind, but surrounded both Mordecai and I in the abandoned church that we called our home.

"A wonderful memory isn't it?" whispered the laughter, its form stepping out from the shadows and into the candlelight.

Its thin black cloak cast the top of the creatures face in shadow, but the ebony gnarled teeth gave away who the unwelcome visitor was. His feet fell softly upon the cold stone floor, advancing him closer and closer to my companion and me.

"What is it that you want?" I demanded, the respect that I had moments ago in my dream evaporating with anger.

The morning star laughed as he came closer, resting his claw upon my shoulders, his grip firming as he began to speak.

"You awoke from your nightmare before I could say what I wanted, my child," he explained. "You and Mordecai, whether you like it or not, have been forsaken by the heavenly forces of God. You both have become my agents through the years, your routine feedings alone giving me the strength I needed to survive, and now I wish for you to do me one last favor."

I scoffed at the request, but Mordecai requested in turn that I be silent. The creature in front of us entranced him. It was then that I realized, dear reader, that Mordecai and his ability to cling to humanity made him weak when it came to Lucifer and his tempting ways. He was manipulated like clay in the hand of an artist, and Satan loved every minute of it.

"What is it that you want?" I snarled. I was realizing that I had been manipulated my entire life into being a dark pawn in the sinister plans of the fallen angel.

"Centuries from now, a child of mine shall rise. He will lead the tribes of the Germanic people, long lost to the times of history, and sink the world into the flames of war. He will successfully control the continent that crucified the lamb, and none shall be able to touch him.

"However, he will lead the people of Abraham into a tribulation they do not deserve. And that is why I need you, Mordecai. I wish for you to save those you deem worthy, rescue those children of Abraham from my infernal flames, for though I may grow strong from their deaths, not all deserve to feel my presence," he said eloquently.

Mordecai nodded with a large smile, glad to know that though he was a damned soul, he could still help those that were deemed worthy. Satan himself smiled, his twisted teeth piercing the veil of his lips, and he turned to me, pointing a dark claw in my direction.

"And you, Asael, will allow the demon that you are to overcome you. You will take those I deem worthy and feed from them, their religious zeal fanning the flames of your true potential," said Satan, maliciously.

"And how, pray tell, will I know the ones you deem worthy?" I requested.

"Follow your heart, for the true Asael remains there," he said, vanishing in a puff of smoke, the smell of sulfur filling the room.

Book Three

The Rise of a Child

Chapter Ten

The centuries flowed like a river into an ocean, and Mordecai and I found ourselves immersed in structures of abominable architecture and terrifying constructs of metal and oil. Industrial smog grayed the sky and polluted the pristine waters that once surrounded us. Creatures of greed and envy infested the streets of a once poor, dark nation, and the world sank into the flames of war and battle.

Our hearts churned with the infernal warnings of a time when an evil child would rise and lead the tribes of a long lost race to prominence, placing the children of Abraham into an undeserved tribulation. My own heart burned for their blood, the curse that gripped it parched from centuries of fasting, but Mordecai's heart yearned to help the people who were deemed worthy in his eyes, in his own mind a fantastic way to have his sins absolved in the eyes of God, and a way to prove himself to the sickly, pale creature known as Lucifer.

We found ourselves in the service of the child, who grew from his humble origins to a powerful leader who inspired the nations, lulling them into awe and pride. He knew of us, long before we knew of him, and he met with us personally before assigning us to our diabolical posts within his concentration camp.

"Welcome, my friends," he said with great gusto.

He stood at average height, his brown hair neatly and perfectly groomed, his brown eyes gazing at our pale skin as we walked closer to him. He stroked his small patch of facial hair on his upper lip, studying us and our movements, and a slight smirk crossed his sunken face.

"My father tells me you are here to help me, Asael," he said with joy, staring into my eyes with the wonder and amazement of a child. I merely nodded to him, saying nothing to the hell spawn that lay before me, his very words leaving a bad taste in my mouth.

"Soon, my race will return from the depths that they have been imprisoned in, and they shall sweep the world like a raging fire. Their strength, agility, and wisdom will ensure victory after victory against the inferior races that try and destroy us," he preached proudly.

"Your race?" asked Mordecai, staring at the son of Satan.

"Yes, the Aryan race," he declared enthusiastically.

"The … Aryan … race," I said softly, the dark voices within me laughing heartily, knowing the truth about the race that this man wanted to bring upon the world

"Do you remember during the Black Plague? You saved a mother from dying?" asked the son of Satan.

We nodded in unison, the truth dancing in my head, but not revealing itself to Mordecai.

"You fed her your blood, healing her and momentarily giving her great strength, agility, and wisdom beyond her years. Do you remember what she did next?" he asked, the slight smirk evolving to a large grin.

"She kissed her son," answered Mordecai flatly.

"Yes, and when her saliva, laced with your blood, entered his system, he was forever changed. His physique became greater, his agility heightened to superhuman levels, and his intellect surpassed that of the greatest minds of his time.

"When he reproduced, his spawn of children experienced the same effects. When they matured, and bred with humans, the budding race that they had become grew like wildfire, only they have been scattered to the winds," explained the man with a grand smile.

My fists clenched as I realized that it was our creation of an abominable race, something that at one time I was very proud of, that would be manipulated to swarm the planet like locusts, destroying and pillaging all who oppose them and their quest for domination. Deep within my dark heart, I began to grow jealous of the thought, knowing that it was truly my own destiny to throw the world into the lakes of fire and rivers of acid that raged underneath its surface. The demon that swam in my festering soul sang with laughter at my thoughts.

"Let's get down to the business. You've both been assigned to the Sobibor camp. There you will find plenty of specimens to feed from," he said with a slight chuckle.

He turned away from us and began walking back to his desk, his black polished boots making audible clicks as he walked casually toward the wooden furniture that housed important papers and documents necessary for our official assignment. His hands worked quickly and fiercely, until they finally rested upon the pieces of paper that would give us all the access required for us to complete our damnable task.

"Here you are, gentleman. Now, if you'll excuse me, I have important work to get done," said the man as he sat down in his leather chair, his hand wrapping around an ebony pen.

"Before we leave, can we have the name of the man we will bring glory to?" asked Mordecai with a quaint smile.

"Call me Mein Führer, for that is what I am to you," responded the man with a smile.

The man who would kill millions had hired us as guards to

watch one of his many extermination camps. He knowingly invited
wolves to protect his unwanted flock, and with that realization,
Mordecai and I left his presence.

❧

Days passed since our meeting with the bastard child of Satan,
his evil presence still clutching our hearts and minds, making us
think of nothing but the false hatred he was forcing on the masses
of people who followed him.

We stepped into our roles as angels of death the minute our
leather-booted feet touched the dirt-covered ground, the eyes of
countless fear-stricken and starving victims staring back into my
own dead eyes, sending a nervous shiver down my spine. I looked at
Mordecai, who stared at the sea of innocent victims as I had, and for
once the compassion that he routinely showed for the human race
was vacant from his face, and his mind was filled with one question:
Has Lucifer played a trick on me?

I smiled, for I knew that our jobs were set in opposition, and
my heart burned for the death of all those who dwelled within the
confines of this prison. Mordecai's mind yearned for the release
of the countless believers who were falsely imprisoned within the
modern purgatory. I knew that no matter how hard Mordecai tried,
my task would be completed far easier than his, for I had legions of
demons in Nazi clothing to help me accomplish the blood bath that
would ensue in the months to come. Mordecai was a single angel in
an ocean of devils, and his greatest foe was also his brother who had
helped him through the centuries.

We marched through the walking corpses and shambling rotting
humans, the stench of decay and feces raping the air as we delved
deeper into the camp of death that would be our pathetic domain
for the short span of our eternal lives. Our pristine black uniforms

contrasted with the pale creatures who scuffed their way to and fro within the confines of the hell that would be their new habitat. Laughter echoed from the barracks that housed the cretinous guards who infested the camp, their gullets being filled with wondrous food and delicate drinks.

My claw pushed open the door, the hinges creaking under its weight. The pungent stench of feces and death were quickly substituted with the sweet scent of delicious meats and rich alcohol, the gray, dreary surrounding replaced by the vibrancy and life that inhabited the small walls of the barracks. The laughter that erupted from the mouths of the malicious guards, once jovial and loud, ceased. From those very mouths that the joyous sound came from flowed curses as they gazed upon the fresh meat that would join their mob of bastards.

"Who the hell are you?" said one, the stench of alcohol exuding from his pores.

Mordecai stared at the drunken guard, his anger cascading over the passive mind that he possessed, his claws digging into his flesh, causing ruby-red blood to erupt from his pale skin. He loathed the heathen bastards who lingered in front of him, drinking and eating their fill as their prisoners wasted away in agonizing hunger. I placed my hand on his shoulder and gave him a look that disarmed the aggression he harbored for the cretins before him.

My heart ached for the men in front of me, wishing to dispatch the amount of pain they had sown upon the countless peasants who dwelled within their camp, and my mind burned for their blood to drip from my lips.

Mordecai fumbled for the documents that explained what we were and what we came to accomplish. He held them with an icy grip that was fueled by the anger he harbored for the guards that flourished and thrived as the prisoners they detained starved and fought for rats to sustain themselves. A gloved hand of one of the guards ripped the crisp document from my companion, and his glazed eyes scanned the document. His eyes widened and narrowed, his mouth contorting to various grins and scowls, and finally he looked at me in the face.

"Nosferatu? You mean to tell me that our Führer, a man we all love and respect, believes in vampires, and actually thinks he hired two?" said the guard, handing the document around to his compatriots, partaking in laughter as the document circulated the room.

Mordecai, bestial with rage, leapt over the table that put distance between him and the guard. My companion's claws dug into the pest's shoulders, pinning him to the wall. His eyes flooded with a violet color as the animal deep within took over, his hatred for the elite sending him into a fury. He plunged his claws further into the flesh of the moaning guard, his claws hitting bone as he glared into the fear-filled eyes of his prey.

"Let go!" yelled the other guards, their voices cracking slightly with fear.

My companion laughed, his teeth expanding into vampiric fangs as his thirst took over. His laughter was silenced as he sank his sharp fangs into the blood-engorged neck of his tense prey, images of the disgraceful acts that Mordecai had experienced throughout his life inundating the mind of the guard. Muscle and sinew tore as my blue-eyed friend ripped his claws through the meat of the pathetic creature in his grasp. Any and all sensation the pleasure-loving cretin had experienced was replaced rapidly with grotesque pain.

"Release him," I muttered quietly, my words heard loud and clear by my companion, who immediately yanked his claws out of the guard gracefully and effortlessly, his drained body slumping on the ground.

"Would anyone else like to question the legitimacy of what it is we claim to be? Our duties are clear, and we are not normal guards. We have been given full authority to do as we please, and it's obvious that none of you could stop us, anyway," I reported, leaving the corpse of their companion to fester and decay in their presence, slowly replacing the vibrancy and life to the gray dreary landscape that was the entire camp.

We departed the barracks that housed the drunken buffoons, the sounds they sang changing from disgusting laughter to mourning screams as they inspected their dying friend. A small smirk came from Mordecai, the effects of the blood he just took delight in coursing through his veins.

"What?" I asked curiously.

"For once, I enjoy being the hell spawn that Cain forcefully made me so many years ago. Perhaps the sins of the bastards of this era have wiped clean my conscience of all guilt. I actually enjoyed ending the life of that swine," said Mordecai, his smirk growing to a large smile.

Chapter Eleven

The life of a guard in the confines of the extermination camp was relatively uninteresting for my eyes. The routine degradations and humiliation of the children of Abraham were but a footnote in a large book of despicable human acts I had seen. The Jewish people moaned in agony as they slowly starved, malnourishment making their blood thin and tasteless, eroding the amusement and thrill of the hunt.

And although this thrill and rapture that I sought was absent, my heart ached each and every night for the rivers of blood that could have been flowing from the wretched creatures that dwelled around me. I quaked with hunger for days, in an attempt to honor the wish of an old friend, until finally the parasitic darkness that gripped my aching heart demanded that I feast. My mind became obsessed with the feeling of warm blood pouring from the veins of my battered and weakened prey, their sacrifice strengthening my ancient limbs, and fueling my ancient life

The numerous peons in pain around me made my veins itch and blood burn, their once-proud lives stripped from them, any wealth accumulated by them ripped from their grasp, turning the shambling corpses into filthy whiners and destitute husks. They were powerless to stop their now inevitable demise and the hell spawn that possessed me would routinely laugh quietly to himself whenever he saw them, slowly wasting away in the camp that was worse than hell. Mordecai, always a creature of sympathy, became the new messiah for these wretched balls of imprisoned filth, aiding them in any way he could. He gave them the rations he received, sending the vile food that seemed like ambrosia to those who appeared the most weak and frail. Their rough-skinned hands grabbed appreciatively at the cleanly wrapped rations of food, caressing the delicate surface as if it were a piece of gold. The sight would always move my companion into a fiery fit of rage and sadness, his mind screaming of the torture and pain he would make our cowardly Schutzstaffel brethren endure, the moans of pain and screams of terror that would erupt from their mouths and saturate the air always making him smile.

He despised the genocidal machine that the Schutzstaffel were a part of, always talking about how Nazi Germany was an insidious parasite upon Europe, demanding that we immediately gut the nation that housed thousands of defenseless citizens imprisoned in the shackles of infernal bondage, the propaganda of the government condemning these very citizens to camps of labor and fields of death.

"It wasn't always like this, Asael," he said. "The Germany we were a part of was once a shining example of how a crumbling nation could explode with amazing potential and strength."

I nodded, realizing that all the things we'd seen the nation dragged through had brought about the desperate acts of a man who didn't fully understand the consequences of his actions, dragging the race of holy creatures through the mud and bringing unjust retribution to an entire populace. Satan must be dancing in his dark palace, watching his puppets twirl and spin in their futile attempts to gain free will and control their fates.

"We can stop this," I said, my voice pungent with benevolence.

"We can end it all. Free the humans who are wrongfully imprisoned here, feast from the Schutzstaffel, and destroy this abomination that has become our nation. It wouldn't be hard."

Mordecai smiled, the charitable words coming from my mouth inciting a riot of thoughts within his mind. His blue eyes became inundated with a maelstrom of joy and mischief as he stared at me, his smile contorting to a devilish grin. His pale hand gripped my shoulder, like old men do when they are about to impart life-altering wisdom.

"It appears the charity work we have done and my humanity have planted a small seed within you, Asael," he joked.

"And may it be burned in the fires of my rage and loathing," I retorted with a smile of my own.

The next few nights were filled with the smiles and cackling of the hyenas who infested the ranks of the devious Schutzstaffel, our own faces filled with the knowledge that we would become angels of death in the coming nights, the darkness of night covering the red mist that would spray into the air as our claws freed the prisoners in the camp by severing the skin and flesh from the bones of their captors.

Mordecai himself even laughed and joked about the eventual demise of the satanic beasts who inhabited the skins of men, commenting on how the sinfully sweet nectar that was their blood would be relished by him with great passion. My delicate friend slowly transformed into the beast he was always meant to be, crazed with desire for the death of the demons that lurked in Sobibor. He cackled with delight as he gazed upon his future meals with eyes of lust, like a lion stalking his prey.

Like they often do, the nights passed by on the wings of time, and finally the moment had come for Mordecai and I to unleash our devilish power against the machine that was the Schutzstaffel. Our minds reached out to those whose minds and bodies were shackled to the camp, their spirits writhing in pain and moaning for freedom. We found the very creatures we were looking for in two men, two ordinary humans who would do extraordinary deeds. We lurked in the shadows, observing them individually at first. Mordecai took the child of Abraham, the one who had been around longer and knew the people of the camp and their tribulations. He and a few others had planned previous attempts at escape and even liberated the camp, but all ended in failure. Mordecai loved him for his heroic bravery and courage, and I too enjoyed his hatred for his enemy.

I, however, observed a Soviet soldier who had been placed in the prison not long ago. He was at first a loner, trying to survive in a harsh world that loved the foolish actions of an isolationist, but when the children of Abraham invited him to join them, he broke down and agreed to accept the help of those who had a common enemy.

When he met with the Polish Jews who had invited him into their lair, I could smell the anger that infested his mind. He stood poised, like a masterful orator in front of a sea of impressionable minds, and with graceful words reported the various things that were happening around the world that surrounded them. The attention of the Polish Jews was captured by the detailed descriptions that were spewing from the Soviet soldier, and when he finished, silence covered the crowd like a blanket.

"Will the partisans not save us?" asked one of the Polish Jews.

"What for? To free us all? The partisans have their hands full already. Nobody will do our job for us," replied the Soviet soldier.

With his simple reply, the soldier had rekindled a dying flame within the half starved and fully beaten humans, turning the struggling spark into the wondrous fire that Leon, the leader of the Polish Jews and the one that Mordecai had been stalking and studying, would use to inspire and influence the men and women who were shackled to the terrifying imprisonment that they faced.

He nodded as the words from the Soviet's lips swirled within his head, the intense mental flames forging a weapon that would inspire numerous uprisings. All Leon needed was a little help.

Nights came and went, and Mordecai and I were left undisturbed by the majority of the camp, until one night a sickly thin creature waltzed into our domain, his black cloak fitting tightly across his weakened body. His black, gnarled teeth pierced his putridly innocent smile, and with a quiet nod he forced us into talking with him. His festering claws embraced my own, the filth and grime from them flooding my pores as he gripped my hand in an iron-tight embrace.

"How are my favored angels?" he asked genuinely, as if he cared about what happened to us.

"We're grand. In fact, we were just about to begin the groundwork for completing both of our tasks," replied Mordecai; an equally putrid grin covered his face as he spoke to the abominable morning star who cursed us with his miserable presence.

"Good, very good. Tell me, what does the future hold for the lovely children of Abraham, Asael?" asked Satan excitedly.

"The children will rise up and attempt to destroy Sobibor," answered Mordecai with enthusiasm, his answer making the smile upon Satan's face widen, the obsidian souls of the Schutzstaffel eventually feeding the emaciated husk of a man that was the morning star.

"And what of your task, Asael?" asked the Devil, his words saturated with contempt and a sense of being let down.

"My task was to feed my inner demon with the blood of those I deemed worthy, correct?" I snapped, glaring at the abomination who fell from grace.

He nodded with a smile, his black gnarled fangs seeping their way into my mind, burning their vile visage into my mind, leaving me even more angry and filled with hate than I already was.

The scent of vengeance and glorious retribution hung in the air as the prisoners of religious intolerance began their fantastic plot to destroy the disgusting bloated beast that was the Schutzstaffel, the demonic serpents that festered in human skins and terrified even the most strong and noble of men. Mordecai smiled with unending glee as he fed the rebellious prisoners his blood, fueling their grand revolution with a dark light that burned brightly in the humble eyes of the tortured spirits that were the children of Abraham.

Like a baby cub with a mother's bosom, the imprisoned Jews suckled with great relish, the dark nectar creating the very creatures that Hitler demanded we spawned. Their civility and fearful minds were wiped clean when Mordecai's blood flooded their system, turning them into machines of chaos and justice. The fragile fighters that suckled from Mordecai quickly turned into minions of hatred and revenge, vengeful spirits bent on tearing the fabric of the Nazi empire asunder. Their hearts trembled to feel the pulse of their tormentors slowly die away, the sweet revenge starting with the small act of delayed self defense against the murder of their religion and race. Their rage and desire for blood fueled the resistance movement that dwelled within the hearts and minds of all those who lurked in the fields of death.

"When does the bloodbath begin, gentleman?" Leon asked, the effects of the crimson substance injecting him with vitality and eagerness.

We both stared at him. The wonderful mix of joy and curiosity springing from our features must have made him feel strange, for he tilted his head slightly at our expression. My mind began to search for the various things that I demanded to be done before the true resistance started, passive aggressive resistance suiting the needs of these fragile creatures more than an all-out assault on the filth that imprisoned them.

Mordecai gazed upon the Jew with wondrous excitement, the

sensation of freedom for the Jewish people building up within the creature. His blue eyes studied the waves of anger that billowed from the human, all nicely contained in a fragile flesh sack of mortality, the icy talon of death lingering over the skeletal husk that had become Leon, even with the frothy nectar that poured like wine from Mordecai's veins.

The next night was the real start of the uprising, for it was the night that I turned the Soviet known as Alexander into an unstoppable darkness that could blot out all of Nazi Germany, covering it with insanity and chaos like a blanket covering a child. I brought him into my quarters, leaving him isolated from all the blood-frenzied Jews who might have tried to help him, and with this isolation came a slight fear that bubbled within him.

"Fear not, Sasha," I said, "I'm here to make you the leader of this uprising."

"Why me? Why not Leon?" he inquired.

"Because he has been tainted by the blood of a lesser being. If I were to feed him my own blood now, he would turn into a vile creature obsessing about a single thought or creature, making him useless to the cause.

"But you, you have been untouched by the blood of Mordecai, and because of your pristine system, you will lead the uprising against the despicable demons that dwell within this field of death," I explained to him.

He smiled slightly, shaking his head after I finished my small speech, and with this act a divot of anger sprouted within me, my claws digging into the flesh of my hands. Blood trickled from the punctures on my palm.

"You aren't the superior being, you parasite. Mordecai is twice the man you will ever be," he spat. "You are no better than the pitiful men that plague us, feeding off our fears. If I were you, I wouldn't feed me your bile, for if I ever get the power you possess, the first thing I would do is end your miserable existence."

And with that lovely threat, I gripped the neck of the Soviet and dragged his mouth underneath my palm, the crimson droplets of blood dripping into his mouth. His muscles tensed at first, his mind thrashing around like a cornered animal, but when the nectar entered his system his muscles relaxed and his mind became clouded and subdued.

"Go, lead the countless children of Abraham who are chained to this place and send them to freedom. Make the guards despise you, taunt them at every turn, and if they lay a hand on you, let the taste of their blood taint your mind," I said with a smile, leaving the Soviet to experience the subtle changes to his physique and intellect alone, for he would forever be alone in the society of mankind.

Mordecai, waiting outside of our modest quarters, looked at me with a vicious grin. His mind screamed with pride as we walked our usual patrol, stalking the outskirts of the camp in the veil of darkness that was the night. He seemed to dance to and fro with excitement as we crept along, leaving me more and more agitated at the adolescent behavior.

"What's made you so excited?" I inquired, irritation saturating my voice.

"Sasha said I was a better being than you," he said with a smile, "and you didn't kill him after that."

"There is a reason for it, Mordecai," I said, a twang of laughter erupting quietly from my lips.

"Oh? What is that?" he asked, all happiness and excitement drained from him.

"My blood, the very substance that will allow him and Leon and a handful of others to escape this infernal place, will change him forever. His personality and views will change, from idealistic to nihilistic, and with that change he will abandon all the things that meant something to him. And the best part is, he won't know why he is doing what he is doing, but he won't be able to stop himself from doing it," I said, my cruelty both astounding Mordecai and making me feel better about the situation.

Mordecai didn't say anything after the most recent revelation festered in his mind, but his mood quickly changed from happy to depressed. His mind swarmed with images of a lonely Alexander, saddened in his isolation, but doing nothing to change his predicament. The pitiful human's mind burned for more blood, yearned to feel normal again, but unfortunately nothing would embrace him and return him to the state of normality that he lusted for with all his heart. In truth, the thought made me smile, the mighty Soviet turning into a defeated bitter specimen, praying for death but unable to find his dark salvation.

Weeks passed by, and I watched with eyes full of pride as Sasha turned into a twisted perversion of the pitiful creature he had been. He carried out his mission, however, wonderfully. He turned the prejudice filled and bigoted Nazi guards into savage beasts of hate, incapable of any real thought other than their hatred. They retaliated to Sasha's taunts by killing various Jews in the camp, a small oversight that was cured by Mordecai feeding their corpse's blood, turning them into shambling creatures that would inspire fear into the ranks of the Schutzstaffel, a wondrous accomplishment on his part.

The Polish Jews in the camp had devised a devious plan, a lovely strategy to assassinate all of the SS guards and walk right out of the camp. Mordecai's blood made them bold, but thankfully Sasha realized that this plan would be near impossible to accomplish successfully, so they created a list of targets instead. Their new goal was to make mass confusion for the auxiliary units, allowing the imprisoned to run into the forests that surrounded the camp.

They toiled long and hard on their list, picking those who were vicious and evil, a difficult task when choosing from a list of demons and snakes. They deemed their targets worthy of death, some thinking that death was too good of a fate for those who made their lives worse than hell.

Sasha said that they would start their uprising tomorrow, during the daylight hours. He demanded that we not help them, and requested we leave the camp for fear that we may betray them. It hurt Mordecai dearly, but I laughed and welcomed the dismissal, giving him a small vial of my blood to strengthen him and anyone else he deemed fit to have the fantastic poison that would be his ultimate undoing.

"I can't believe they asked us to leave," said Mordecai, wounded deeply by the lack of trust Sasha showed.

"They asked nothing. Sasha demanded it," I corrected. "However, there is nothing saying that we can't make their jobs a little easier."

"How do you propose we do that?" asked Mordecai innocently.

"Leave it to me; soon the SS will be nothing more than obsessed apes," I said, disappearing into the shadows of the night.

I remained in the shadows for quite some time, until I came across a weakened prisoner. She wouldn't make it through the night, and if no one did anything for her, she would experience a painfully slow death that would send ripples of pain through her system. It was a fate she didn't deserve, so I took it upon myself to allow the cold grip of death to embrace her faster.

I walked up to her, my icy cold hand rubbing her shoulder as she slumped against the wall of the small hut that was her dwelling. Her brown eyes welled up with tears as she recognized my face, knowing what was about to happen. Salty, wet tears strolled down her face as I embraced her, the weak heartbeat of a dying women singing a quiet ode to death as my fangs pierced her rough dry skin, the blood from her veins slowly seeping into my mouth.

"I'm sorry," I said, as I rested her dead body on the ground, closing her fear-filled eyes as she drifted to whatever God she worshipped.

Her blood coursed through my veins as I walked toward the barracks that housed the vermin who tortured and beat these innocent humans, still filth and garbage in my eyes but undeserving of the treatment they had received. My clawed hand pushed open the door, and when my pale visage entered the room, a dead silence hushed over the crowd.

"What do you want, Nosferatu?" asked a guard, his finger jabbing my chest.

My icy hand gripped his wrist, breaking the bones of the weak guard. I threw him outside of the barracks, the strength gifted to me by the blood of the dying prisoner sending him flying toward the chain link fence that wrapped around the perimeter of the camp. He swung at my head, both times making contact with my jaw, both times his knuckles crunching as they met with my undead skin. He screamed in agony as the pain of his broken bones pulsated through his body, only to be silenced by my hand on his throat, lifting him into the air. I sent him sailing through the darkness of night, his skull cracking as his thick head hit the chain link fence, the pattern of it impressing upon his face as it dug into his pitifully rough, dirty skin. My face contorted in sheer ecstasy as my heart burned for his divine crimson nectar, the warmth of his blood sending cascading shivers across my pristine body. The demon within me cackled as I ripped the fresh corpse from the filthy ground, bringing his insipid skin to my thirsty lips. My fangs pierced the pitiful creature's neck, his meaningless essence slowly flowing down my throat, bathing the demon that dwelled within me.

The other guards looked at me with eyes of wonder and fear, their jaws opening as my eyes returned to their normal color, the luminescent violet leaving my pupils as the blood worked through my system, turning my saliva into a dangerous poison. I smiled as I walked closer to them, their minds demanding they run and scream, but their bodies not responding to the various commands.

"Enjoy spending the remaining years of your life obsessing about the demon that entered your ranks. Always yearning to see me, and feel my presence, only to feel empty and never know how to fill the deep hole that lingers in your soul," I said with a sadistic smile.

I slit my wrist, blood flowing from the wound freely. I placed the lips of each of the guards on the wound, the blood trickling down their throats, giving them a wondrous feeling. When all of them had drunk from me, I spat into each of their mouths, the poisonous spit of a vampire who had just fed. Slowly but surely they would become ghouls, and with this terrifying transformation would come the successful uprising of the camp known as Sobibor.

Chapter Twelve
Revelations

With the fall of Sobibor, and the new race of dhampir Jews that Mordecai and I spawned, the child of Satan demanded we speak with him. His brown eyes met the icy blue stare of my companion, and the dictators' mind sang with contempt, loathing the fact that his true father's pawns failed him in their simple task.

"How could you fail in constructing the very simple designs I gave you?" he demanded.

"With all due respect, we did not fail you. We created your race of dhampirs, just the subjects we chose were not the specimens you wanted," I said, my mind assaulting the human's mind with the images of what occurred nights before the uprising began.

"You turned the slimy prisoners, the lesser beings and filth-encrusted worms, into creatures with power beyond their wildest dreams," he replied. "If that isn't failing, I do not know what is."

Mordecai clenched his fists at the insults to the poor children of Abraham. He saw them as brothers, a noble people with a great belief, a culture he once belonged to before he himself was forcefully made to enter the darkness of eternity with a diabolical curse. He loathed the child that practically ruled Europe, and his thoughts rested on the nefarious things he would do to the Austrian man before he had the chance to destroy him.

"Do you realize what tasting our blood once, but never again, does to a person?" I asked, smiling as I looked at the hell spawn.

He look at me as he shook his head, his eyes burning with anger.

"The infected are never the same again. They'll change views, opinions, and personalities. Sasha Perchesky, the leader of the uprising, will never be the man he was when he was forcefully shoved into that camp, none of the prisoners will. I know for a fact that the second he and the group of others escaped, he ditched them and took whatever they had of value before departing. Men of reason become beasts, and beasts in sophisticated society usually get put to sleep," I explained.

Mordecai, knowing this all along, looked horrified as I explained the fates of those who survived the uprising, paying even more for the superfluous choices of long-dead ancestors. The hell spawn smiled as he realized we didn't technically fail him, but instead killed those he was trying to kill, just a little more cruelly.

"Excellent work then! All is forgiven!" he exclaimed as he placed his hand on my shoulder, squeezing it gently, an attempt at a friendly human gesture.

"Hold on a second," I said, "Those who did survive—those who tasted my blood and became aware of what we were—will be unstoppable. They are something more than just the dhampirs that you wished to create. They are full-fledged vampires bent on tasting your blood."

He removed his hand from my shoulder, his brown eyes studying my own, trying to determine if I was lying or not. When he realized I wasn't, a look of bewilderment spread across his face, its very presence like a wildfire feasting on dry brush.

"That's impossible," he said smugly. "They started the uprising during the day."

"The weakness to sunlight doesn't come right away. In fact, it doesn't come until after they have died, which for all of my children at Sobibor, should be happening right about now.

"I'm afraid your little quest for domination and spreading the Aryan race will be very short lived," I taunted, a wide smile spreading across both Mordecai's face and mine.

The familiar stench of sulfur filled the room as Hitler glared at both of the dark parasites who inhabited his domain. The sound of hands clapping impaled the room as the pale-skinned, black-cloaked visage of Satan slithered into our presence, the hell spawn that came from his loins bowing before the king of temptation. His black claws embraced the hand of Mordecai, causing the vampire to smile with glee as he saw the morning star.

"Father, you told me these two would ensure all my plans came to fruition. They've done nothing but sabotage my constructs, kill my men, and strengthen my opposition!" yelled Hitler, his foot stomping the ground like a pathetic child.

Satan smiled at his kin, his black claws leaving the soft flesh of Mordecai's hand to embrace the face of his offspring with the decayed digits of his hand. He ruffled the hair of the Austrian dictator like so many fathers do, and with a soft slap on the cheek, turned away from the hell spawn.

"My child, you are far too trusting. Your mission that you put upon yourself, one covered in death and torment, was a terrible fate to have incarnated for yourself. You were supposed to unite Europe, not leave its people bathed in blood and caked with the ashes of war," said the morning star sympathetically.

"But … Father… you told me to spread your influence. I was only doing as you requested," explained Hitler, a small tear strolling down his face.

"I told you to conquer the continent that crucified the lamb, not eradicate the descendants of those responsible for his death. While all wars have casualties, no leader should ever demand the death of innocents unless backed into a corner. They did not deserve the torture and pain you inflicted upon them just yet," said Satan, his cardinal eyes studying his offspring.

Hitler stared at his father for what seemed to be an exceptionally long time, his small mustache twitching occasionally as his mind focused on the chalk-white skin of the lithely built man before him. His hand fidgeted by his side, the sweaty palms of the human patting the fabric of his brown pants, leaving traces of dampness that erupted from his nervousness. Satan himself glared at the hell spawn, his crimson eyes examining the failure of a child that Hitler was.

"You don't even realize what your actions have caused me. Heaven, and the power of God, besieged the black gates of hell. They slaughtered countless demons, and if it were not for the first murderer, who knows what my fate would have been!" said Satan serenely.

Mordecai and I shifted in our stance, the air in the room palpable with the anger that pulsated from the morning star, and the fear of the Austrian dictator. Silence reigned in the room for some time, until finally the seed of Satan spoke again.

"Father, how can I redeem myself in your eyes? Please, anything you want, I promise to succeed at getting it," said Hitler, his sweaty palms shooting out to grab the black, decayed claws of the morning star.

Satan smiled, patting the hands of the Austrian dictator. The devil looked at me, a sinister smile spreading across his sadistic mind, and within my own mind flashed the fateful demise of the pitiful hell spawn that infested the room. I smiled as well, the sight of which made Satan grin widely.

He slithered his hands to rest upon the shoulder of his son, the black claws entering the flesh as if not tangible or real at all. Tears rolled down the child's face as he saw the hand of his creator travel toward his chest, his beating heart pumping faster and faster as he awaited the terrifying demise that awaited him. Satan turned his open hand into a frightening claw, his black claws wrapped around the beating heart of his kin, whose eyes were inundated with fear and sadness.

"Please, Father, don't do this," begged the dictator like a mangy dog.

The morning star twisted his hand one way, and then the other, ripping the beating organ from its resting place. Blood dripped from the mass of flesh and tissue, covering the floor with its presence. Mordecai smiled with uncanny satisfaction as he saw the corpse of the man he loathed slumped on the floor, his skin quickly turning gray and cold as if he had been a corpse for months. Mordecai stared in horror at the grotesque organ still beating in the decayed grip of the tempter of man; his blue eyes glued to the dripping blood that soon started to saturate the carpet, the dark fluid pooling around the bare, festering feet of the demonic male clutching the heart.

"What happens now? Germany will fall without its enigmatic leader," said Mordecai

"He shall become a recluse. I'll have the world of men see the image of Hitler for a little while longer, having him die far away in a bunker somewhere," said Satan, nudging the cool corpse of his child.

"And what of us? What shall we do?" I asked, my eyes not leaving those of the corpse, the dying eyes of a worthless mortal that benefited only his people.

"You shall travel to the wondrous continent known as America, the land of the free and home of the brave," Satan said with a smile, winking as he did so.

"The sinful souls of those you wish to reap, I assume?" I said with a smile of my own, knowing exactly what Satan was after.

Satan moved closer to me, his smile unwavering as he read my mind, his presence in the dark canals of my memories like an uninvited friend at a social gathering. He peered deeply, drinking in the darkness, and when the thoughts came rushing toward him, he stepped back slowly, nodded, and then smiled wider.

"You don't like working for me, I see," stated Satan, his red eyes singing as the words left his mouth.

"No, I don't. The benefits are terrible and the pay is lacking," I said, smiling.

"You wish for some kind of benefit then? This can be arranged, my friend. Sadly, though, only you can receive the gift, Asael. Mordecai's body would deteriorate rapidly if I were to give him what I will give you.

"Are you sure you want what you are asking?" asked Satan, his black talon of a hand resting upon my shoulder.

I looked at Satan curiously, and when he began to smile, I couldn't help but nod. The devil had never given us anything but blood before, and I must admit that my mind yearned to receive whatever it was that he was willing to give me. He smiled as he read my mind, the craving of power insatiable inside the hollow shell that was my heart.

He pushed up the sleeve of his crimson cloak, his black claw slicing a long incision into his pale skin. He smiled as the slight pain from the wound rippled through his body, the sensation foreign to his immortal body. He held his wounded wrist before me, offering me a taste of the black blood that bubbled out from the cut, to which I obliged him begrudgingly. My lips surrounded the cut, and I delicately lapped the liquid that oozed from the wound with my tongue, the sickeningly sweet taste rushing down my throat.

My head began to swim as I ferociously sucked the blood from the cut, my eyes turning violet as I fed from the dark immortal in front of me, his blood strengthening me far more than any other creatures had. My mind raced, my heart danced, and my vision blurred as the twisted temptation to feed became stronger, and with its powerful hold on my mind it forced me to taste more of the black oil that was Satan's ambrosia.

"Yes, keep going," was all Satan said as I drank his veins dry, the power he possessed becoming my own, the voices of the dead screaming in terror as they slowly saw my transformation complete.

When I finally released the limb of the pale devil, my eyes rested upon Mordecai, who stared at me with fearful eyes, not sure of the beast I would become after tasting the black nectar that oozed from the devil's veins. I smiled, assuring my friend that I was the same creature I had always been. Only it was a lie, for the blood of the fallen angel left me stronger than I could have ever become. Memories that were alien to my mind flooded the dark prism that was my skull. Visions of death, birth, and rebirth cascaded before my eyes with their terrifying magnificence. Skills and information that would have never been available to me flourished within the weapon that infested my skull, the burning blood of the devil causing me to be reborn amid the winds of change.

I evolved, rapidly and without effort, to a powerfully evil creature that knew no equal. My powers, infinitely numerous and splendidly useful, wracked my soul with their presence, tortured my mind with their capabilities, and raped my eyes with their sheer awesome potential. My mind danced outward and my dark brain burned with temptation. It gripped the hearts of those who dwelled within the building. Quickly, and without warning, the blood-pumping organs of my unknowing test subjects began to beat to the rhythm of a terrifyingly fast song, their chests burning with pain and their veins aching with activity.

I smiled with a delicious grin of satisfaction, the awful power of destroying countless mortals by mere thought springing a tingling sensation that danced all over my body. Mordecai, however, chuckled in disgust as he saw the sickeningly satisfied smile that I wore, and shook his head in disapproval.

His mind screamed the nagging words, "You can't use that," over and over again, accompanied by protests of the terrifying possibilities of human life being destroyed en masse. I laughed bitterly, turning my concentration onto the powerful parasite that stood before me. His heart began to burn and bake under my stare, the dark blood in his body scorching his veins with acidic cruelty, causing him to double over in pain. He moaned like a desperate fool, his mind begging for mercy, and though I wanted the madness to end, my mind continued to ravage his form. His eyes screamed in pain, their blue color fading to a burned black, the veins in his face scarring the pristine skin that covered Mordecai, his hair quickly falling out of his head.

When I finally summoned the strength to rein in the vile beast that my mind had become, Mordecai lay on the ground, his dead heart unable to pump the required blood to restore his normal appearance. He arose, a charred husk of what he once was, and with pain still plaguing his body, limped toward me. I expected anger, rage, or even hatred toward me and my inability to control the dark powers from Satan, but instead I was met with a cruel smile and the dirty feeling of being forgiven. Guilt, the most alien sensation known to me, coiled its slimy skin around my mind, constricting the thoughts that crawled within my skull with its greasy presence.

⁖

I could tell our journey into the twenty-first century, a century that would be inevitably wracked with terror and pain, would be a long and arduous one. The new powers that I now controlled would cause even more complications. To say the least, I was filled with dread as we departed the presence of a rotting corpse and the incarnation of evil. Terrifying events lingered on the horizon, and I was powerless to stop them from becoming real as we bravely stepped once more into the breach.

Book Four

Modern Times

Chapter Thirteen

The twenty-first century. My prediction of terror and pain was right, for we are only ten years into it and the country of our inhabitance has already been plunged into the fires of war once again, and terror now rules with an iron fist. New racist ideologies replaced the old, and the American Dream quickly became infected with new layers of nightmarish fear and pain. People prayed for death more and more with each passing moment, and the lingering thoughts of anguish infested the mind of my immortal friend.

He plunged himself into the dark waters of their madness, succumbing to the suicidal thoughts of the numerous creatures that plagued his mind. He begged for a reason, a cause, an ideology, anything to help those who needed help, but he found himself amid a swarm of problems and never knew where to start first. He yearned to make life better, utilizing the immortal touch that Cain bestowed upon us so many centuries ago, and he quickly realized the major problem that faced humanity. It wasn't disease or poverty, but instead he realized that it was my mere existence that gave the humans their mental necrosis.

My companion for the ages, my savior from all corrupting evil, had finally found my bloodlust unbearable. He found my very movements vile, and when he could no longer take the rage and darkness that emanated from my heart, he simply walked out of my life and into the urban jungle that was America. His departure from my existence, though it pained me dearly, was a welcome one. Ever since the tangy blood of Satan passed my lips, Mordecai demanded that I use my newfound power to help those who could not help themselves. Instead, I found myself in sheer ecstasy with his absence, experiencing the numerous cities of death that dotted the landscape of North America, adding a few more corpses to their rising death toll.

One night I found myself traversing the labyrinth of streets of one such city. The stench of urban decay infested my nostrils as I walked through the dark streets of the rotting necropolis known as New York. Filthy humans lined the dirty alleyways, moaning in hunger and clinging to the hope of charity from benevolent strangers, their grimy faces screaming for attention from the numerous cretins who passed their resting places. The grimy fingers of a skeletal walking corpse grabbed the linen of my clothes, begging for the currency of the realm that lined my pockets.

"The only charity I will give you is to not end this existence of yours," I spat, my mind reaching out into his, the power bestowed upon me from the devil infecting him with a demonic disease.

Immediately after the words left my mouth, the fool started screaming vile obscenities and broken lines from Scripture that he had heard during his tenure at church, the throwback to a life he once possessed before he was thrown out onto the streets after losing so much in the tumbling economy. To be honest, the whole thing made me smile. Yet here I was, shrouded in the darkness of a new age and completely alone with the powers of a God, and I was wasting precious moments destroying the life of a pathetic human who begged for charity.

I was rather afraid that this would sadly be my life without

Mordecai, haunting the various alleyways and torturing the homeless. The thought quickly evaporated, however, when I sensed the presence of immortal blood, thinking that perhaps Mordecai was about to try to come back into my life. Sadly, I was mistaken, and the ensuing moments changed my life forever.

"Asael?" the creature said. I barely heard his hoarse voice with my supernatural senses.

Before me stood a rather tall specimen of what appeared to be the human race. His eyes were blue, but behind them was a lingering presence that seemed unnatural. He stared at me with a smile, and it wasn't until I saw his teeth that I understood what I was dealing with.

Now, my loving reader, I will explain what happened to the other members of the original coven. You already know what happened to Nafretiti, Mordecai, and Ephraim, two succumbing to the eternal darkness and one leaving me to rot in eternity, but you do not know what happened to the other beasts I called my brothers and sisters. If you have read any vampire novels, you would have read of a world teeming with the vampiric curse, and while that it isn't necessarily the case in reality, there are more than just a few of us. My brothers and sisters decided to depart each other, the strength and wisdom they once had due to Cain's presence splintered and diluted.

A few of them had walked into the sun, your people mistaking them for zealots setting themselves on fire in protest or strange miracles. But the others, those who could not or would not end their lives for whatever reason, spawned a new breed of vampire. Strangely, it appeared that Mordecai and I were legends among this new race, a fact that I found most flattering.

This abominable progeny of my brethren, a weak creature in comparison to me, moved with the grace of an undead angel. He glided toward me, the pitter patter that accompanied footsteps absent from this immortal beast. The closer he came to me, the stronger the sweet scent of death and watery tears became; it was the unmistakable scent of a fresh vampire. His blue eyes, reminiscent of Mordecai's, studied me for a brief moment, attempting to probe the mind of the devil that apparently haunted his generation's dreams.

"We all thought you were a myth," he said with a twang of immaturity.

His sapphire eyes burned with excitement as we stood within the dark alleyway, the screams of a crazed homeless man burning within his ears. He motioned toward the street, his mind pleading with me to follow him, to meet more of our kind who would be dying to see me. The idea was an interesting one, I'll admit, the chance to be around numerous predators that shared my thirst for blood.

"There will be dozens of blood sacks for you to drain, if you want," bribed the young vampire, his American slang for human ringing in my ears, summoning a quiet chuckle from within me. I nodded to him, intrigued to discover what kind of blood sacks gathered around powerful beasts of darkness. His mind apparently was ripe for the picking on the subject.

Underneath the radar of humanity, a subculture of vampires had grown, and with its growth came a new following of hopefuls. Think of it as a biker gang, where you have to prove yourself among them before you can join them. Unbeknownst to the blood sacks, however, was that the chances were slim of joining this gang.

We departed the homeless shouter, my lovely parting gift to him spreading quickly and efficiently throughout his entire system. The young vampire led the way, his grace and skill apparently abandoning him as he tried to navigate through the crowds of people that engorged the streets of New York. I chuckled quietly to myself once more, reading his thoughts and picking the place of our destination out of a raging sea of images and sentence fragments.

Without even trying, I focused on the nightclub that would be our resting place for the night. Blackness surrounded us, and in moments we were waiting outside the palace of dancing and social encounters of the twenty-first century. Techno music poured out into the streets, making the waiting patrons dance in line with excitement. My vampire guide, startled by the bizarre power that I had demonstrated, looked at me in wonder. I nodded to him, my obsidian eyes telling him to do what was needed for us to gain entry into this spawning pool of the modern world.

He approached the large bouncer at the door, his mind linking itself to the blood sack who guarded the entrance. With a vivacious nod, the bouncer stepped to the side and allowed us entry, his mind cowering in fear when he realized who and what I was.

After I breached the threshold, I gazed upon a new Sodom that was filled with impure thoughts and filthy intentions. The perfect nest for a vampire to hide, their presence being masked by the sexual energies of the numerous blood sacks who filled its walls. The youthful vampire tugged on my hand, his cold flesh pulling me toward a group of gothic looking specimens, the absence of a beating heart filling their chests. The posse gazed upon their young brother with a warm smile, fangs flashing in the black light that swarmed the club. When they felt my presence their smiles vanished.

"Who is this? I don't recognize his scent," said one of the females. A thick accent saturated her words.

The posse encircled me with curiosity governing them. Pokes and prods covered my body and mind, the futile attempts of children trying to read the thoughts of a God. My own mind reached out, the invisible hand of my power clutching all of their dead hearts, causing them to beat once more, the churning of stagnant blood shooting pain throughout their eternal bodies. It was at this gesture they all recognized me, for they all experienced dreams as humans did, and I infected their nightmares.

The female who spoke out was the first to gain full composure. She appeared to be the oldest and strongest of this little coven, garnering the respect of those around her. She stared at me with teary eyes, the pain still wracking her body, her mind refusing to let it affect her. A quick probe of my own showed they had no discerning curse to them, each being identical to the last in their ways of dealing with their existence.

"So, the legends are true," said one of the females, her voice shaky with excitement.

"Legends?" I asked, curious as to what my brethren told their sons and daughters.

"Our leaders, before leaving us, told us that there was once a great coven. Led by the one named Cain, and through him our leaders were brought into existence, twelve creatures of terrifying power. Asael, Mordecai, Ephraim, Nafretiti, Naphtali, Levi, Manasseh, Asher, Judah, Reuben, Daniel, and Benjamin. Our leaders informed us that each member of the coven, every single one of them, had something that set them apart from each other, ranging from clinging to their own humanity to hearing the voices of the dead, and though they were cursed, they lived in perfect harmony and peace.

"The coven prospered until the youngest of them, Asael, came into existence. Something vile and evil lived within him, and he aimed to disembowel the entire coven's innards just because he loathed the rule of Cain. It is told that he lied in wait, biding his time, hoping for an excuse to rise against his father," said the female, her blonde hair swaying as she enthusiastically told the story.

"And an excuse arose, for Ephraim, the weakest of them and most cursed, died by the very fangs that created him. Cain drank his blood and sent his soul to the flames of hell, where he was swarmed by the fallen that he had killed," interrupted one of the males, his peculiar New York accent covering his words in a lovely veil.

They stopped their story, looking at me with the eyes of a mystified child, seeing I had grown bored with their tale. They realized that they were telling me information I already knew, and when that realization came, their pale faces blushed with fresh blood. Their minds buzzed like a beehive with questions of their own, but the eldest vampire, their apparent leader, had gripped their tongues with her mind, telling them all to be silent. She looked into my black eyes, and I could feel her lingering presence within my mind. Her hazel eyes focused, all her strength placed into the simple act of reading my ancient mind, trying to get a solid grip on what I was thinking, and yet it was utterly futile for her to even attempt it.

"It's no use, child," I said, bringing my clawed hand to brush her raven hair to the side. "I'm far too old and far too powerful for a few parlor tricks to work on me."

"It's strange; we can't read your thoughts or feel your presence, even when you stand before us. Yet, there is another creature that we do not know, who has the immortal touch, who is older than you, and he shouts for us to come and find him. He begs nightly to be killed, his mere existence a burden to himself, yet nothing will kill him," said the oldest female, her hazel gems still locked with my own.

"You must be referring to Mordecai," I said plainly, his abandonment of me in a new age leaving me a little bitter toward my ancient ally.

"Indeed, Mordecai. Why does he not just walk into the sun, if his existence is so terrible?" asked one of the males.

It was at that moment that boisterous laughter erupted from me, filling the entire room with its presence, drowning out the sound of the thunderous music. The new coven cowered away from me, not sure what had possessed me with such amusement to summon such a reaction. With eyes full of tears, I finally motioned for them to draw closer to me, assuring all of them that it was okay. Soon after their evacuation, they scurried back, their minds bathed in curiosity and terror.

"We do not die so easily in our age, or my generation, for that matter. In fact, I do not know that our death is even a possibility," I stated, my black eyes falling to the floor as my mind drifted to all those who came before me, their existence wiped away from this realm with the death of Cain, the netherworld not even holding their souls.

The new coven had requested I stay with them, as a mentor and guide through the rough waters of immortality, and in return they'd give me a link to this era. Overwhelming madness stormed the horizon of my mind, and the only thing keeping it at bay for these generations was my ability to connect with my friend Mordecai. His absence threatened to pluck the strings of my sanity until I became a husk of near limitless power, alerting the world of a terrifying beast that had been hidden within plain sight for millennia. But with the presence of this new coven, I intended to keep the cloud of madness at bay once more, learning from them the new customs of America and hopefully throwing to the wayside my complete loathing of the blood sacks who danced within the walls of my new domain.

Once I had settled into this new life of mine, the youthful vampires came to see me quite frequently, hoping to push out nuggets of infinite wisdom here and there with our talks. The eldest among them would routinely ask if she could sit and talk with me, her eyes always filled with the curiosity of a new student.

"The others look to me for guidance … yet I myself know nothing of this curse that we all share. What am I to do?" she confessed to me one night, her eyes filled with red tears, her voice trembling.

She wiped away the crimson droplets, trying to regain the composure that abandoned her for that brief moment. Her hands shook as the sadness that infected her gripped the heart that sat within her chest, her finely-manicured nails shining in the dimly-lit club. I looked at her with pity, the face of a youthful teenager weighed down by years of turmoil and ostracizing. Nowhere in her mind was there an ill thought or feeling toward any living or dead creature. She respected the source of nourishment that swarmed her as well as her younger brothers and sisters.

Her leg shook as she sat beside me, the music moving through her with exuberance, the vibrations of her leg causing her bracelets to rattle together. I found myself staring at her, the youthful beauty that usually fades with age still clinging to life enthusiastically with her.

"How old are you?" I asked.

"When I died I was seventeen, but that was in 1793. August 17, to be exact. I only remember the day because it was my birthday, and the pain that I experienced on that day was immense," she explained.

"Pain of death?" I asked.

"No, it wasn't that, though it did hurt when my heart stopped working. No, instead of physical pain, it was emotional abuse," she said.

She informed me that the vampire who turned her tortured and maimed her living family, and feasted upon her friends. It is a common tactic among our kind to destroy the will and happiness of their targets to make them easy prey, but this bastard decided to then turn his prey into a daughter, hoping to seal her love with his eternal kiss.

"He forgot how much I cared for those who were my friends and family, forgot how fiercely loyal I was to those I called my friends, and didn't realize that even in death, I would still see him for the weak beast that he was," she explained, her pale hands clenching to fists as she recalled the story.

A tear strolled down her cheek, the painful memory of her death flooding her mind with the memories of those she had grown attached to dying, the painful lesson of abandoning human relationships being learned all too late for her.

"Whether you realize it or not, you know what you can do for your coven," I told her. "You've experienced the painful loss of those you care about that most of these vampires will never know. You are the oldest among them, by many centuries, and know things of this curse that they would never learn about by themselves. I know you've seen the others of my generation, asked them questions like you do with me, and while they may have been more sympathetic and loving toward you, they left you with more questions than you began with," I said.

Silence grew between us for a few brief moments, and with its tender presence, my eyes wandered toward her once more. I noticed that her thin frame was shaking, like an addict who yearned a fix, and I could tell she hadn't fed since my arrival. Her hair, which when I arrived was filled with body and shine, was dull and flat, and her skin, once pristine and well cared for, had grown blotchy.

"I have a question of my own, if you do not mind. Why have you not fed yet?" I inquired, hoping the reason wasn't because of some misplaced love for the *Homo sapiens* who surrounded us.

She looked away from me, her clenched fists loosening to open palms, her mind woozy from the lack of blood. I could tell she yearned for the taste of our ambrosia, her mind screaming in anguish from its absence, and yet she refused to allow the red liquid to pass her lips. She sighed, and looked at me, her eyes weighed down by her immortal years.

"When I drink, the memories go away," she said, her hands trembling at the thought of a clean slate and blank mind. "The faces of my parents, the love for my brother, it all flutters away like birds in the winter. I've already lost them; I don't want to lose their memories."

Her mind screamed in sadness, the image of the beast that turned her ripping the flesh of her younger brother from his blood-drenched bones, the moans of pain coming from her mother as the fangs of the demon pierced her flesh and drained her of the frothy substance that dwelled within her veins. These were the memories she didn't want to lose, and though I understood the feeling of not remembering the pleasures of mortal life, the clarity and pain of these memories made even me shudder in fear. But for her, these memories made her remember what it was like to feel the loss of a loved one, and though she needed the blood to survive, she wanted to make sure the victim she picked was worthy of death.

"All humans are worthy of death," I said, my minds wandering to the numerous souls dancing in the club that we were in.

"But not all are worthy of my touch," she said, a small smile embracing her.

With that last sentence and thought, she pried herself from her seat and, like a feline huntress, pierced the crowd of prey. She slowly was lost to me in the seas of sinful dancers, and with her absence I scanned the crowds for those worthy of my own touch, a touch that would forever silence their beating hearts and lay them down in a bed of earthen soil.

The minds of those around me, the simple brains of the blood sacks that infected our domain, all focused on one single thought. Their sexual energy loomed in the flashing lights and warm climate of the club, and though the various fantasies and fetishes they all harbored intrigued me, one specimen drew me in more than any other could. Her hips swayed beautifully to the music, and I could tell by the way the male thoughts of the club revolved around her that she was an object of lust and affection for all those that gazed upon her.

In short, I had to taste her blood.

My mind reached out with the dark powers gifted to me by the morning star, and with their ability I invaded the minds of those who thought about this vixen, her beautiful hair and gorgeous eyes possessing the minds of my gender, making fear and shyness grip even the most outgoing and successful mate in her vicinity. My black eyes gazed upon her, the rhythmic dance and wonderfully hypnotizing eyes looking right back at me, beckoning me to approach her, a small smile spreading swiftly across her face as I slowly walked toward the object of my desire.

I, too, pierced the crowd of prey like a dark predator, my gaze never breaking that of my chosen blood sack. But, sadly, the closer I ventured to my chosen target, the stronger my urge to observe the wondrous specimen before me became, and though I wanted to taste her, to feel her touch, my mind would not allow it. So there I stood it seemed, for the first time in my existence unable to kill a human because she was too radiant to destroy, and yet I yearned for her blood.

Chapter Fourteen

The lights from the club switched from the abyssal black that danced from the purple bulbs to bright white, signaling the end of this night. The blood sacks infecting the club all winced at the sudden change, the vampires in the club standing out among the *Homo sapiens*, unchanged by the drastic alterations in light. The sight brought a small smile to my face, predators swimming in the waters of urban entertainment, ready to snatch up their chosen prey and devour the lovely nectar that flowed through their veins.

My eyes spotted my vixen, the creature that my heart yearned for, and my smile grew wider as I saw her slipping out the back, entering a sea of shadows as she walked into the dark alley that dwelled outside her choice of exit. My feet carried me into the darkness of the alley, the stench of modern life swirling around me, her perfume lingering in the midst of it all. The clicking sounds of her booted feet sang out into the night, alerting the predators of death and evil to her presence.

As I stalked my prey, my mind began to scan the wet brick and cold asphalt, sensing for any forms of life above or below us. Subtle heartbeats from rats and insects mingled with the ebb and flow of the modern city, until they were replaced by the presence of another predator. One like me, but far younger, the hunger exuding from him like sweat. His mind descended into madness as he focused on my prey, his heart burning for her blood, skin crawling for her touch.

"Hello, lovely," he said seductively.

Her mind screamed with terror, a fact that brought a fanged smile to the face of her predator. She instinctively turned around and ran, only to run into the presence of a far more terrible monster. My ancient limbs encircled her, hugging her close to my own body, her perfumed skin rubbing up against my own as I looked into her coffee eyes. The young vampire glared at me, standing his ground and demanding for his prey to be returned to him.

"She's mine!" he snapped, his fangs growing in anger.

I placed my lovely prey to the side, my lips burning for her blood and her mind praying for salvation. The vampire stood his ground, claws growing by sheer will, fangs bared and ready to pounce. The sight of the predator brought an irresistible sense of pride for my race, the creatures of the night that had spawned from my brethren's loins, and though I was proud of the brave acolyte, his blood lust for my prey made him an enemy.

My mind reached out, the invisible darkness spewing forth from the powerful entity that swam within my skull, sticking its greasy claws into the brain of the vampire before me. His snarling stopped for a brief moment when he realized who I was, only to return again when he learned of my plans with him. I chuckled loudly as I disappeared from view, the power of an ancient fueling my gifts. The lovely prey that I had saved began to scream, thinking she was alone with a beast bent on sexual deviance and murder.

The creature himself turned around and around, sensing my presence but not actually knowing where I lurked, fear and hatred bubbling from the deepest regions within him. And just as quickly as I disappeared, I materialized right behind him, my white fangs piercing immortal flesh, the dark blood gushing from his veins into my open gullet. My hand caressed the skin of my immortal prey, my eyes raging with violet luminescence, focusing on the wonderful woman cowering by a Dumpster in the alley, her screams filling my ears. And then I noticed something interesting about my vampiric appetizer.

His unbeating heart, in the waning moments of his life, started to pump once more. For a brief second, between life and death, he was human again. The presence of Cain left him, and in those short moments, his mind screamed out with heavy guilt. The vampiric sociopath had returned to the light of humanity. Before he died, a single, transparent tear rolled down his cheek, and with that one drop of humanity, he died.

I returned my gaze to my other prey, the gorgeous human who had entranced me in the club with her beauty and grace. Her eyes peeked through her shielding hands, the torment of not knowing what was happening too much for her to bear, but when she finally saw the fate of her attacker, her mind squealed with a strange mixture of joy and fear. His pale flesh draped across my ancient arms, his head lolling back in a lackadaisical fashion, the life from his veins drained from him completely.

"I can't begin to thank you enough," she said, prying herself away from the Dumpster and into an embrace with her savior.

Her scent wafted into my nostrils once more, reminding the bestial demon that clutched my heart that it forever yearned for the blood of these creatures. My mind lamented for her crimson blood, yearned for her tantalizing touch to die on my skin, never again embracing the flesh of another creature for all eternity. Her mind, focusing on the dead creature at our feet and the mysterious stranger who saved her, squealed with a new sense of enjoyment out of life. She vowed to be kinder to those around her, and change the way she dealt with potential mates, for embraces with death often change her kind drastically.

"I'm afraid your plans to change have come too late, for death has not flown by you with his wings of ice. Instead, he has come in a far more toxic creature," I said, my arms locking her into the embrace that she was once so enthusiastic to give.

She struggle and squirmed, at first. But when she realized the futility of her effort, she began to cry and beg for her life.

"Please, I've done nothing to you; there is no reason to kill me. Take my money, my car, whatever it is that you wish, just please allow me to live!" she cried, the tears flowing like raging rivers from her brown eyes.

I'll admit, dearest reader, that I did consider not killing her. I debated with myself for what felt like an eternity, wondering if this beautiful blood bag in my arms would be worthy of the immortal touch, eternal beauty, and unwavering grace. But while I debated this, the mind of this creature sang out, demanding her God to allow a righteous bolt of retribution strike down the devil that threatened her, and she prayed for the immortal touch of her divine savior to rescue her from the flames of hell that followed the beast that held her in his arms. With all these thoughts, I considered her unworthy of my gifts, unworthy of the power that darkness had given me.

I shook my head, a smile on my lips sending waves of dread through her system, her blood becoming a lovely cocktail of terror and anger. My fangs grew in hunger, the demon in me laughing with glee as he was about to be drowned in the crimson blood of another morsel. I forcefully shoved her head down, revealing the tan skin of her soft neck, and with predatory grace, my fangs entered the veins of my object of desire. She moaned, pleasure mixing with pain and fear, her head rolling back in ecstasy as the blood left her veins and entered my system, the shock of human blood sending warming chills across my body.

As the blood flowed freely from her to me, her mind slowly flashed through her life, the normal experience that her kind went through before their death. She showed me her driving her car to a young man's house, an evening of bowling and movie watching before them, she showed me this same man going too far and betraying her trust forever, and finally her mind rested upon her family, the love for her brothers and sisters greater than any love she had ever felt for anyone else. The single tear, the single release of her soul, dripped from her face and landed upon the bare asphalt, the pumping of her heart stopping at the exact moment that the tear splashed against the hard surface.

Days passed since I feasted from the alleyway vampire and the object of my desire, and with the passing of the acolyte vampire came numerous questions from the others of my coven around me. They demanded to know the motive behind my slaying him, the sensations I experienced with the taste of his blood, and what happened when he expired, the sight of their generation dying something none of them had ever seen.

"Why did you end the existence of my fresh child? The curse barely graced his veins," demanded the leader, her youthful face hiding the emotions of rage and fear, wanting to condemn me but powerless to do anything to end my existence.

I stared at her usually flawed skin and coarse hair replaced by the pristine features of a vampire who just fed. Her eyes, often clouded and puffy, glared at me with sharp brilliance, the green flecks in them contrasting wonderfully with the brown iris. I smiled at the elder creature, and with that smile I began to explain myself.

"You refuse to feed, the taste of blood washing away your memories, yet when you feed, when the memories are replaced with the dark mist of forgetting, how does it make you feel?

"And the hunt, the stalking of prey down urban streets and dark alleys, the heartbeats of humans filling your ears, the unknowing thoughts of a creature about to die, doesn't it make you love your nature?" I asked the elder before me, who was standing slack jawed at my questions.

The other coven members whispered among themselves, the words blasting within my unnatural ears, their hidden secrets revealed to me with relative ease. They felt no grief for the passing of their newest brother. They loathed his existence and the way he treated others of our kind. With their approval of what I had done, I stared at the elder, who nodded as she too heard the whispering voices.

The other members of the coven dispersed among the crowds of club-goers and dancers, leaving the eldest vampire among them isolated with me in the bowels of the club. The music pumped and made our minds swim, forcing our bodies to acclimate to the conditions around us, drowning out the modern music that we found unsettling.

The eldest among the coven walked through the shadows, her hazel eyes shining with a preternatural glow. She looked upon me, her eyes staring intently upon my own features, studying the skin that encased me and the black gems that rested in my eye sockets, power and wisdom dwelling behind the obsidian orbs.

"You have questions," I said plainly.

"Yes, if you don't mind answering them," she replied, her mind sorting the swarm of questions that raged within her mind.

"Ask, and I shall answer."

"What was it like, killing the acolyte?" she asked, the question rolling off her tongue with ease.

My mind burned with the question, the demon in me fondly remembering the taste of the blood and the sensations it induced.

"You know the thrills and chills you get when feeding from a human?" I asked, her response an enthusiastic nod. "Imagine feasting from thousands of their kind, and experiencing those very same thrills and chills for each of them. The power that flows through our veins will be transferred to whoever feeds from us."

She thought of the reply carefully, trying to imagine the feeling of draining another with the vampiric curse and gaining their power. She couldn't fathom the possibility of killing one of her own kind, much like a human claims they could never harm another. I found her weakness upsetting, reminding me so much of Mordecai, but then I realized that things were different for these youthful vampires. Their blood was still wet with humanity, and so I forgave them for their inability to do what was necessary.

"I can sense you're hungry," I said, smiling at the oldest vampire amid the young ones, the final trappings of humanity still clinging by mere threads to her bones.

She nodded, biting her lip to try and forget the pains of hunger. Her mind screamed with the memories of her dead family, the memories that made her refuse to taste the tantalizing flavors of blood. She looked at me, her hazel eyes yearning to know what to do, like a child looking at a parent for guidance. She stepped closer to me, her immortal mind wanting to remember her family but her eternal heart wanting the blood of humans, and the closer she got the stronger the sensation of pain emanated from her.

"We are predators, as they are. Memories are fleeting, but the hunger is forever. Feed, and get a sense of normalcy," I said, turning from her and exiting the room, leaving darkness as her only companion.

With my departure, I took to the streets of the city that surrounded me, the cold pavement teeming with souls for the harvesting, oceans of blood flowing in their veins. The thoughts and desires of the mortal men and women around me were like a sitcom, the various fantasies and fetishes flowing freely into the air, snatched from the air by my immortal mind.

One creature's thoughts, a lone female, sang out amid the roars and screams that thrashed around her. She sat on a stoop, staring at various people walking around her, trying to guess what their various goals and lives were, the simple pleasures of a lonely woman. She repeatedly combed her long, flaxen-colored locks through her fingers, only to allow her hair to drop and fall back into place. Her innocence, which was in abundance, was a rarity among her kind of this era, and she reminded me of Mordecai.

At first, I'll admit, I thought it was Mordecai. Her thoughts were focused on ways to help a friend who had been tormented by depression and suicidal thoughts, but her human frailty, something that Mordecai lost and replaced with immortal cowardice, set firm in my mind that she was in fact special. Though her mind had plenty of things to worry about, for some reason death was lingering among the seas of memories and oceans of problems.

It was at that moment that my heart started to beat for a brief moment. Pain ebbed and flowed through me. The terrible sensation I had learned to forget so long ago returned with a vengeance. The dark voices, still crawling within my skull after all these years, pleaded with me to take her, feed from her blood and allow her mind to lay at peace. But the demon lurking within my heart, the true me, wanted to experience her for all time, have her by my side for eternity.

Sadly, the heart beat the mind, as it does with your kind as well, and I found myself waiting for the opportune moment to welcome her to the eternal world of vampirism. But she didn't move, she just sat there on that stoop and watched people for the entire span of her night. That is, until she spotted me, saw me with her own eyes. She recognized from my skin color that I could not be human, or at least not a normal one. My visage terrified her. She recognized my pale skin as unnatural, and though I terrified her, she only smiled at me and nodded, the polite innocence within her refusing to be rude to a scary stranger.

She sighed, once or twice, and looked down at the cellular device gripped tightly in her hand. She yearned to talk to someone, yearned to have back what she lost only months before, but sadly her phone remained motionless, the image of a sunset the only thing staring back at her. With defeated sadness, she finally pried herself from the stoop, the scary stranger she spotted still standing there staring at her. With a sheepish smile, she turned away and walked into her apartment building.

But that wasn't the end of my night. I refused to let this encounter end this way. I thought of her soft skin pressing the button of the elevator, her pink lips popping to make various sounds as she waited for the mode of transportation to arrive. The dark powers gifted to me by Satan fueled my body to appear within her room, the unclean apartment of the innocent girl I had moments ago observed. And my preternatural senses heard the keys rattling on the other side of the door, a quiet song emanating from the voice that stood just behind that door, and finally the door swung open.

And yet, it wasn't the girl I had just seen. The girl before me was tan and had brunette hair. Her hair was straight and far longer than the innocent girl on the stoop. Her green eyes stared at me, horror filling them as she saw the beast in man's skin in her living room. Her hand rummaged through her purse for something to use as a weapon, and with a feeling of satisfaction gripped a can of pepper spray, aiming it directly at my black eyes.

She uttered a silent prayer for protection, something that made my undead self smile. I dashed toward her, vampiric quickness exceeding the ability of human comprehension, and before she knew where I was, my hand was upon her throat. Stifled screams struggled to get out, the claws of my ancient hand gripping her tightly. The scent of fresh urine danced around her, her mind losing control of all muscle functions, and with the warmth of the liquid dribbling down her leg, a small tear danced down her cheek. Her mind kept praying, begging to not be sexually assaulted or abused in any way, saying that I could have any and all that I wished just so long as I didn't harm her.

"Do not worry; rape is the last thing upon my mind. Your death, however, is first," I said, my serpentine tongue licking her cheek as the last words slithered out of my mouth.

My fangs pierced her flesh, the warm blood lazily entering my mouth. She tried to scream, tried to make a sound of any kind to alarm someone, somewhere, of her passing. The warmth of her blood, the purity of it, sent my mind reeling as I drank more and more, the beating of her heart growing weaker and weaker until it finally refused to pump the delicious nectar in her veins anymore. Her limbs went limp, her body cold, and her hair and skin lost its shine and vitality. Her body looked as though it had been decomposing for quite some time, the lovely effects of being drained by an immortal.

The blood of the roommate made my heart sing with joy, for I would need all my power if I were to craft the very best vampire I could out of the flaxen-haired female who was swiftly walking down the hall. When she arrived at her door, I could hear that lovely jingling sound of keys once more, and the click of a tumbler turning to unlock. With a successful click, the door swung open to reveal a seemingly normal apartment.

As she always did, she peeked into the room of her friend, and there she saw her long-time friend lying peacefully in eternal slumber upon her bed, and the sight brought an innocent smile to my flaxen-haired friend. She turned around, and continued to go about her routine when coming in for the night, ensuring the door was locked as it automatically did when opened and closed, making sure all the windows were shut, and checking her phone once more for that small glimmer of social contact she so desperately wanted.

But this time, her phone had a voice message. She squealed with excitement as she saw it, not remembering her phone ever ringing, but then again she could've been too busy with her routine or people watching to have noticed, she reasoned. With almost natural instinct, she brought up the message and began to listen to it intently, only to have all excitement drained from her as the voice on the other end became a voice within the room.

"Hello, my friend," I said, appearing from the shadows and materializing before her.

Her eyes grew wide, her mouth hanging agape, and she became motionless. Fear gripped her heart and mind, making it impossible for her to move an inch from her place, the perfect prey placed before a predator of unknown villainy. Her mind demanded movement, pleading with her lame muscles to make her flee, but they refused to cooperate, the taint of evil staying their hand.

I smiled as she abandoned her basic motor functions, her current status turning her into a frightened sentinel gazing upon my visage. She was terrified, but so are all your kind when they feel my presence, the very essence of evil exuding from my every pore, the touch of the morning star teeming in the palm of my hand. My mind invaded hers, the little nuances of thought that permeated within her brain becoming known to me and it was at that moment that I realized that turning her into what I was would be torture to her. She wanted to die, perhaps not now, but at some point in time she wanted to experience death and see what the afterlife held for her. But she was a human, my dear reader, and as I'm sure you've guessed by now, my true self demanded she became the parasite that I was.

"Please, just don't hurt me. You can have whatever you want," she said, her hands outstretched in an attempt to put a barrier between her and myself.

"But what if what I want is to do something that would harm you for centuries to come? Rip away what makes you *you*, and replace it with something that contorts your thoughts and desires into something bestial?" I said with glee.

She stared at me in confusion, her arms dropping to her side and her head cocking to one side. Her eyes were misted over in thought, trying to figure out what it was that I was talking about, and it was at that moment that I ended her world and invited her into mine. Without hesitation, I was upon her, the warm feminine clothes brushing up against me as I embraced her in my arms. She screamed, the terror that she felt moments ago paling in comparison to the sensations she was now experiencing, the thrill of the feast exciting me to no end.

My fangs sank into her flesh, the blood from her veins gushing into my mouth and down my dead throat, the humanity of my prey sliding down and rejuvenating me further. The sweet taste of innocence that I had not tasted in decades exploded in my mouth. She was rapidly losing blood and though I would have loved to experience all of the morsels she had within her, I pried myself away from the blood sack in my arms, blood dripping down my throat and onto her sickly pale chest.

"And now, my child, you shall become the first of my spawn," I said, cutting my wrist with a fang, the long-dead blood oozing out into her slightly opened mouth.

The foreign substance sprang through her system, resurrecting my dying prey with every drop. At first she sat there, lazily allowing the blood to slowly enter her mouth, but then the infernal hunger that we all feel eradicated her loss of ambition, sending her to grip my wrist and forcefully take the blood from my veins. Her eyes, once a dull blue, shone with violet intensity as the blood circulated through her system, my demonic seed taking full effect at last.

"Welcome, my child, to eternity," I said, prying her away from my wrist and helping her up to her feet.

"Call me Lilith," she said, wiping away the black blood that dripped from her lips.

With the creation of Lilith, all fears I had about the future and my ability to stay sane slowly seeped away, for though the coven was a reliable distraction, Lilith would prove to be a creature that was reminiscent of me more than any vampire I had known. With her, all things seemed possible, and eternity with a coven of children suddenly became tolerable.

Chapter Fifteen

Bubbling with enthusiasm and a foreign euphoria, Lilith had replaced the thoughts of the afterlife with ideas of immortality. Almost immediately after the curse had filled her veins, she burned for knowledge, wanting to understand all around her. Her mind was purged of all contempt for immortality, finding every aspect of it intriguing.

She stood silently, her eyes opened wide and her hands rubbing her temples. I scanned the mind of my first child and quietly chuckled as I saw the dark voices had begun speaking, a shocking experience for all parties involved. They crawled around her mind viciously, tapping on the bones of her skull begging to be set free, only to thrash and rage in hushed whispers about the past of the devil that turned her. But as quickly as they had come, the voices abandoned her, silence ringing in her ears.

The silence continued to ring as she focused upon the sleeping roommate who lay in the next room, the head of my child tilting to one side as she stared at the lifeless corpse under the covers of a warm bed. She crossed the room, the tapping of sneakers upon hardwood floor dancing from her feet, and when she came to the door of her dead friend's room, she placed a loving hand upon its wooden surface. She could sense the blood-drained body already decaying rapidly, the stench of death releasing itself into the air and billowing outward, seemingly staining the white surface of her barren walls with their taint.

A small tear rolled down her cheek as she felt the absence of a beating heart, the life of an acquaintance being the first of many down her long dark road of eternity. With a pale finger, she wiped away the tear, the stain of red washing over its surface. It wasn't sadness that she felt, but instead an odd sense of death embracing her. A slight pain burst through her heart, something I originally mistook for her first death, but as quickly as it had arrived it seemed to have disappeared. The sensation caused her head to snap upward, her eyes fixed firmly upon my own, fascination filling them.

"What was that?" she asked, a dainty hand placed upon her heart in remembrance of the pain.

"Perhaps that was the death of your heart, but for some reason the vampires of this generation do not seem to go through the same things I went through when I first turned," I said, my own hand touching my heart in remembrance of the immense pain I felt.

I focused my mind on hers, the images of my turning swarming the fresh slate that was Lilith's vampiric mind like locusts. She experienced the same power I did, felt the terrible pain, and when the images stopped, enjoyed the same breath of relief I enjoyed all those years ago. She smiled, enjoying the simple fact that she would never have to experience the first death.

Her mind quickly ditched the new memory of her pained heart, and stormed around the idea of her newfound hunger. With its realization firmly in her mind, the return of the dark voices stormed as well, sending her clawed hands firmly into her temples in a desperate attempt to rid her of them. They whispered things of doom and death, of power and pride, until finally she could no longer take their presence.

"How do I silence these damn demons inside my head?!" she yelled with bestial rage.

"Simply drink, and they shall leave," I said, extending my hand out to her.

I felt her soft hand slip into my own, and with great satisfaction I led my new friend into the darkened streets of the city, hoping to feast together on the blood of those unaware of what we were. Her flaxen hair shone in the rays of the moonlight, and her appearance was that of an angel, the curse of my blood gifting her with an unnatural grace that seemed to bounce in every step.

Her hunger burned and resonated outward, infecting all those around her with its very presence. My own mind began to waver in its contentment, the ripples of the dark voices stirring in the dark recesses of my skull. I shook them off, however, and led my child into a dark alleyway reeking of human scum. They gazed upon Lilith with an eerie sense of reverence, as if an angel descended from the heavens had come at last to help them rid their lives of misfortune and bad luck. I smiled as their thoughts danced freely into my mind, but the smile only grew as I observed Lilith play into this illusion.

At first she truly was angelic, cleaning them and offering gentle words that soothed their battered souls. But when one reached out to touch her, to embrace the angel before him, she snatched his hand and sank her fangs into the greasy flesh of the unlucky man. Those who watched became sickened and horrified as their companion was quickly drained of life, flung to the ground like a useless rag doll. But her feeding didn't stop there, dear reader, for she quickly attacked another poor soul and began draining him of his blood, the warm nectar spewing from his veins and snaking down her throat.

When she finished her second helping of blood, the others scattered and escaped the fate that would have befallen those that stayed. Her mind lay silent, the dark voices placating it with the presence of fresh blood in her system. No longer did the painful sensation of hunger radiate from her. It was replaced by the feeling of serenity and inner peace. I felt her soft, dainty hand slip back into my own, subtle pressure squeezing my palm as she looked up at me, her brown eyes shimmering in the darkness of the moon, and a small grin appeared upon her face.

"Would you like to meet your brothers and sisters?" I asked softly.

She nodded, wanting to feel the presence of those closer to her own age and strength, intrigued by the feelings they would bring. I smiled at her inner thoughts, for though they were closer to her age, her power far exceeded their own.

We entered the music-drenched habitat of the club, my first born taken aback by her vampiric senses, the pounding sounds of the music scratching the inner most regions of her skull. I chuckled softly to myself, the ancient curse that flowed through our veins making old sensations feel new for my lovely Lilith. The beating hearts of the blood sacks who swarmed us made her freshly fed mind swim with desire and new hunger, but instead of hunting those around her she merely clung to my side as we approached the coven of children, her brothers and sisters in eternity.

"It appears Asael brings with him some fresh meat," cooed one of the males among the coven.

As quickly as the words left his mouth, my mind forced him to his knees, blood from his victims regurgitated onto the black carpet of our dwelling. His throat burned with agony as the blood spewed from his mouth, an entire night's feast wasted on the onyx floor.

"This is not a human, you imbecile," snapped the eldest as she approached Lilith.

She stretched out a hand, which Lilith politely grasped and shook lightly. The eldest vampire looked upon the creature before her, and immediately sensed the ancient curse that was thick within her veins, the humanity rapidly dying as it was replaced by the curse of Cain. The other vampires couldn't feel her strength, the curse itself not fully sticking to their blood yet, decades only having passed since their embrace into eternity. They all welcomed Lilith, and like little kids do with a new friend, asked her to go with them and play in the shadows of the night.

When the children left, it was only the eldest and myself still lingering within the blood sack-filled club, their heartbeats singing to the rhythm of the music pumping in air. A smile spread across the colonial vampire's face, but her mind didn't reveal what she found humorous. She stared out into the sea of *Homo sapiens*, and the smile only grew wider.

"Do you think they know?" she asked, referring to the humans before us.

"Know what?" I responded, ignorant to what lay within her mind for once.

"That we walk among them, that there are those who make their most deadly weapon look like a child being tickled? That infinite power is at right in front of them?" she asked, her smile almost reaching ear to ear.

The questions she posed had often plagued me in my more youthful days, when plagues ran rampant and wars raged on for decades. The truth is that up until recently, the idea of vampires was relatively rudimentary and usually consisted of the same formula, creatures who drank blood but could never truly think. With the spread of our curse, the creatures we are came into the forefront of human society, when one of our kind wrote what your kind took as a fictional account of a Transylvanian nobleman coming to England. That is when our species slowly started creeping into the minds of humans.

I shook my head, trying to not think of the numerous liars and blasphemers who claimed to fill our ranks. The colonial vampire continued to study the oceans of humans dancing, the thought of humans masquerading as our kind summoning an irresistible smile from the vampire.

"Can I ask you another question?" she asked, her mind shifting from humans to her own existence. I could do nothing but nod, for she would speak regardless of my answer. "How have you survived this long, when others of your generation have walked into the sun or disappeared?"

My face contorted into a scowl, the question summoning the memories of Nafretiti and Mordecai, two creatures better left dead within my mind. But with their resurrection into my thoughts, the answer became obvious. I scanned her mind, wondering what it was she wanted to hear and whether or not my answer would please her, though I'll admit I cared little for her feelings.

"Through the years I've always had at least one creature who enjoyed eternity with me. One vampire or familiar who would keep overwhelming madness at bay, even if they contributed to it at times.

"Without companionship or camaraderie, our mental hold on reality erodes quickly and we soon lose our grip on reality. With my companion, Mordecai, or my love, Nafretiti, I had no reason to walk into the sun or disappear from view," I said, the words barraging the colonial vampire with an icy sting.

She had no companions and felt no camaraderie with those among her coven. She led them and ensured they did not destroy themselves with their bloodlust, but she felt no real connection to any of them. Had they disappeared from her life, she thought, she would never miss them and feel no real difference.

"And if we lack that camaraderie and companionship?" she asked concerned.

"Pray that you find it eventually. You are young, my friend, and have centuries before the taint of madness graces your mind. And if you feel the presence of madness, kill the numerous blood sacks you find swarming around you. Give the greatest gift we can give them, our pain," I said honestly.

She had more questions, but I was tired of playing mentor. I left her to her own devices and her numerous questions, making my way toward the darkness of night to traverse the cold streets of this modern abomination of skyscrapers and metal. The memories that flooded me brought about an urge to find my companion who had walked out of my life, if nothing more just to see him.

The darkness inside my mind reached out, infecting the night sky with its blackened wings, scanning the numerous thoughts of those who infested New York. Violent screams, moans of pleasure, and studious thoughts came swarming in, and eventually the careful plotting of a guilty conscience came shuffling into my mind. His thoughts, wavering with hunger, revolved around the usual plans to help those that needed it.

"Mordecai, your saintly ways sickening me still," I mumbled to myself.

He had apparently taken refuge in an abandoned home, turning the gutted structure into his tomb, rarely piercing the threshold of the door. His mind was sickened with hunger, and it left a foul taste upon my tongue. The creature who helped me for so long, the vampire who now tried to hide his presence from me with such effort, had become plagued with the hunger that afflicts us all, allowing it to fester and stew for such an extended period of time that it spewed its presence into the air and infecting others.

After following the scent, I found myself outside the decrepit building that harbored my friendly parasite. I smiled as I stared at the modest dwelling, its chipping paint and termite-infected wood adding a wonderful charm. I ascended the small steps that led to his door, the rusted knob squeaking loudly as my hand grasped and turned it, the hinges creaking with age as the door swung open.

The scent of hunger only grew as I stepped in, but its scent changed slightly as I grew closer to my target. For what I first thought was the desire for blood rapidly changed to a desire for food, the human desire to feel normal. I scowled at the thought of Mordecai progressing further into humanity, but the scowl quickly evaporated as I found myself in heart of my friend's tomb. The sight of a dying child danced into my eyes, the unfortunate prey for an immortal of unyielding hunger.

"Asael ..." whispered the darkness. "It is so nice to see you again."

"Mordecai?" I asked, the longing for my old friend soaring in my heart.

"Not quite," said the voice, a cacophony of laughter erupting around me as the voice fell silent.

From the shadows burst the visage of a creature I never wished to see again. His black skin and piercing blue eyes assaulted my vision. I was unable to look away from the abomination before me. The tattoos that crisscrossed his body blazed with brilliance, their unnatural qualities burning into my eyes. He had been restored by his protector, strengthened by the morning star, and allowed to roam free on the Earth once more.

"The world has forgotten us, my child," said Cain, his voice sending chills down my spine.

Though it had been two millennia since I had seen him, the anger that I felt so long ago quickly returned. My claws dug into the soft flesh of my palm as I squeezed tightly, hoping the anger would dissipate with the pain. His thoughts invaded my own, and with their dark presence came the feelings of death that I longed to never experience. My heart pumped, my brain seized, and I was completely unable to do anything to stop the sadistic bastard who had begun to torment me.

"Oblivion came when the last drop of my blood entered your mouth. The lies and half truths I spewed to your brothers and sisters

were slapped into my face, and my spirit lingered in the flames of
hell as I watched what our kind put themselves through, the spread
of my curse in the veins of dozens of cretins who did not deserve
such a gift.

"With your death, Asael, a new age for our kind will be realized,"
said Cain maliciously.

My body was wracked with pain, the obsidian claws of an
equally powerful enemy twisting in my thoughts and contorting
my frame. He smiled with satisfaction as he saw his once destroyer
squirm like a pitiful insect caught in the greasy fingers of an evil
child. My mind screamed in lamentation, pain causing it to sing for
help. Boisterous laughter swirled around me, and I could feel his
voice scratching around inside my skull, his inky presence seeping
into my mind once more.

And then, when death was on the very cusp of taking me into
the flames of hell, the pain was replaced with the overwhelming
presence of something familiar to me as my own flesh, the perfect
steps of an ancient predator gliding from the shadows and into the
fray. His blond hair shone with brilliance in the moonlit room, his
fangs pristine and sharp, his blue eyes enraged with memories of a
murdered brother.

"With your death, Cain, I shall find peace," said the vampire,
his fangs piercing the black flesh of my father.

I watched as the blue-eyed vampire, the very same creature
I had spent all of my life with, devoured the blood of the first
murderer, history repeating itself in a brilliant fashion. I rose to my
feet, grasping the wrist of the black-skinned bastard who tormented
me with such relish moments before, sinking my fangs into his soft
flesh. I began to drain his blood just like I had all those years ago.

Mordecai stared at me, the second death of Cain having cured
him of his curse, and for once he knew the way I felt. After centuries
of trying to change that which he could not, he finally understood

the guilty pleasures of having no guilt, and the thought brought a small grin to his face. His thoughts swam within my own, and for brief seconds I knew that he would forever be at peace. But with this realization of peace for my friend came the horrifying realization that never again could we interact with each other, the taste of freedom and scent of darkness too strong in my system. The realization must have hit him as well, for a single crimson tear dripped from his eye.

"Good-bye, Asael. May eternity treat you well," he said before he backed into the shadows, disappearing into the night.

Weeks passed since the encounter with Cain, and ever since that moment I began to look differently at those around me. No longer did I consider them children, the curse barely clinging to their blood, but instead I realized that these were the vampires of a new age. This age would be one where Cain no longer held any sway over what they did or how they acted. I also found myself booming with pride as I witnessed my spawn aiding the colonial vampire in her valiant effort to help the other vampires. The camaraderie she longed for appeared at last.

"I see you've helped the lovely leader of this coven tend her flock," I said.

"It needed to be done. She's a wonderful vampire, but her knowledge of our curse is lacking, and since you refuse to join us, I stepped up," she said with a smile.

"Had I stayed and joined the ranks of your coven, I would've turned into what Cain had been to me, a tyrant who strangled his companions with his very presence. I'd much rather watch our kind spread and thrive than wither and die as I watched," I said as I stared at my spawn, her features shining in the dimly-lit club.

"But you just made me, and I've learned nothing. Where are you going that's so important?" she asked, demanding an answer from the person that condemned her to eternity.

"You've learned all there is to know about our kind, my dear. There are no great mysteries, no wondrous fascinations. You drink blood, and you live forever, you have no special powers or great gifts that all these vampire novelists these days write about," I said, a small smile skirting across my face as I realized the last part may not be true for Lilith.

My blood flows through her veins, which also means that Satan's does as well. This creature before me could very well hold hidden powers and secrets within her, for her heart emanated the dark taint of the morning star, something the others of her generation did not.

"So this is it? An eternity of hunting and killing pathetic mortals who don't hold a candle to my power?" she asked, the sad realization of her new life firmly sinking in instead of just floating at the top.

"Walk the life of a vampire, live it, and spread our curse to those deemed worthy. For years from now, I shall return to this music-drenched habitat. Your brothers and sisters were baptized with imperfect blood, but you and your children were baptized with the blood of a dark god. With our blood, perfection must be reached," I said, the small smile growing to a wide grin.

Lilith didn't quite understand what I meant, but it was to be expected from one so young. The thought of destiny and creating more vampires doesn't sink in for a few years, when the brand-new experiences become routine and dull, and an excuse for why you still live instead of walking into the sun becomes needed.

I left that night wondering what the future would hold. I wandered for hours through the dark streets of a modern world, confused as to how my ancient self could ravage this new age.

My grin practically reached ear to ear when I thought of what my eternal future held, and when the pieces fell together to create the masterpiece that was my ultimate destiny, I was fueled with a purpose far greater than any Mordecai ever had.

The End

My dear reader, I want to thank you for reading this lovely life of mine. I shall admit, it is far from complete, and the beginning seems a bit strange. Details are skewed, and I'm sure you were left with a sense of confusion in some parts, as is to be expected for some of us. Eternity does play tricks on the mind, and I'm afraid the more recent events of my life are easier to remember than those in my vampiric infancy. But, now I'm making excuses.

Endings have always been hard; any novelist or author can say that. Beginnings are the easiest part of any story, for all one must do is take a step forward and be brave enough to speak out to spin a tale. Everything that has transpired in this story is the truth, and I did not fabricate any of it. If I had, I would've ended it with a happy ending, perhaps something like Lilith and Asael settle down and pop out a few vampiric children of their own, live eternity with big, stupid grins and pretend that everything will be okay, numb to their endless hunger and their inability to truly love and experience the most basic of human sensations. Sadly, this isn't the way things happen, for even with vampires nothing will ever be okay for long.

Endings are difficult. There will always be holes that I, as an author, cannot explain, events that seem fake or made up, and because this is the ending, it's all supposed to add up to something and be meaningful and leave you with a new outlook on your own life. Lovers of my book, if there are any, will always complain and moan about one thing or another, such as how I portrayed my species as powerless humans with a thirst for blood and an endless life.

But that is what vampires have always been, dear reader. Originally, we were seen as corpses of a fallen loved one, rising from the dead to feed from our relatives. We evolved from that when Bram Stoker, a lovely vampire with a penchant for writing and exaggerating, came up with a fictional account of his own life, much like this journal of my own. We progressed further along our path in the eyes of your kind with the help of a lovely woman named Anne Rice, who to this day I love and adore with all my unbeating heart. Her vampires remind me ever so much of my friend Mordecai.

And yet, no author has pegged our kind completely. While Mr. Stoker and Anne Rice have come close to piercing the veil of truth, they fail to encompass all of our kind. Some, myself among them, love to kill and feel no sorrow for the deaths of your species. Does all of your kind weep for the cows that are slaughtered so that you may feed? I think not, dear reader. It is unfair, I find, that you should demand our kind to do the same every time we take one of your lives, for what are you to us but cattle?

But I find myself on a tangent, and that is something that would be detrimental to this ending. Some of you will be wondering why I have chosen to end the book this way, and the answer is simple. I do not know what the future holds, this is a true memoir of my life, and to say that things are over in every aspect would be a fallacy. I know that Lilith does go on living, I know that Mordecai comes to terms with his curse after a millennia or two of wracking his mind with torment, and I know that the colonial vampire continues to lead her coven. These are the only things I know, for it has only been a few months since I finished this memoir, and not much has changed.

Now, I know that some of you may want to know more, and please don't fret. I will release another memoir in time, describing the chunks of time I left out in this one, for my presence can be felt in all eras of time since my turning. I bid you farewell, and I pray that we never meet on the street, for I shall be the last thing you see, and my laughter the last thing you hear.

Sincerely,

Asael